Baby

EMMA HILL

Published by Emma Hill, Writes

emmahillwrites.com
First edition
First published 2020
ehw003

Written by Emma Hill
Cover by Jo Walker - jowalker.com
All rights reserved
The moral right of the author has been asserted

Set in Palatino 12 pt

ISBN: 978-1-5272-6335-2

A NOTE ABOUT THIS BOOK

Baby Girl has been written for readers aged 13+.

This book contains storylines involving emotional and physical abuse, as well as a backstory of sexual violence.

If you are affected by the themes or action of this book, and would like to discuss how you feel with someone, Childline offers advice and support to anyone in the UK, aged 18 or under, whatever your worry.

They can be reached online, or on the phone:

www.childline.org.uk
0800 1111

To Tim & Ted – the best things in my life

"I'm just going to write because I cannot help it."
Charlotte Brontë

CHAPTER 1

My alarm is bleeping in my ear - I fell asleep next to my phone *again* last night. This means it's time to get up, stand up.

My slept eyes are dry and sticky. I've got a textbook pressing in my face cheek, after falling asleep doing homework – also again. Dressed in yesterday's school uniform, I roll over to the edge of Nan's spare bed. The springs clunk and clink under me.

And there she is.

"Ah… boo!" I say.

Like every morning, I pretend to be surprised to see her there, awake and waiting, like she is every morning.

Chloë giggles. She smiles. She drools. She fangs her travel cot - gnawing on the hard top. Making marks in the plastic, with her one tooth.

I can smell her nappy from here. It's

hanging heavy, swinging from her bottom, the weight of it making her wobble. I don't like how uncomfortable she must be, her skin getting sore. I deal with it, before I get close to thinking about sorting myself out.

"Mamamamamamumumum," is the gentle sound that Chloë makes, as I change her. It's like a song.

Nan says Chloë is calling me "Mum", when she makes that sound, but I don't know - how does Chloë know what the word mum means, to know I'm Mum to her? Nan says that's not how it works.

My phone beeps – group chat.

SHANNON: It's Monday…
DERREN: I don't like Mondays
TOMMY: *typing…*

Typing Tommy - you wait and wait and then a one-word answer comes through. And it means, well, nothing:

TOMMY: Yeah.

Man of few messages.

I think about replying, finding a GIF, sending a pic of Chloë's full nappy hanging off her little bum, to cheer them all up. But Nan's now speaking from the other side of her spare room door:

"Get moving." So, I get on with it, get dressed, ignore my flashing phone and that normal teenager life. It's not worth the hassle from Nan. I don't care about Mondays anyway - all my days are the same, now Chloë's here.

I start getting changed. Chloë's rolling on her tummy, happy, in a clean nappy. She's making the start of little grumbles and gripes – sounds that mean she's getting hungry. I need two minutes to finish dressing, sort out my face crease and scrape back my hair. So, I tap up that nursery rhymes playlist she likes.

I shuffle play. Wheels on the Bus comes up first. Chloë grins and sings:

"Mamamamamamumumum."

She is looking, waiting. She is hoping I will join in with the track and I can't resist those eager dimples. I listen to the beat and perform for her, while pulling on fresh socks:

"The wheels on the bus go round and round,
Round and round,
Round and round."

I speed up my delivery and throw in more words, it's nursery-rhymes-meets-the-club:

"Wheels fix up, on the big red bus,
Go round and round and round and round,
All day long – hear me now!"

3

Chloë giggles. I pinch her cheeks and give her a kiss. We are happy, until Nan bellows from her kitchen:

"Missie!" That means our breakfast is ready. Nan gets grumpy, if we don't appear immediately, on being called to her serving up food. So I get a wriggle on.

Nan is spick-span. Hair up, bootcut jeans, slight heel on her favourite brown boots, cream top. She has blonde hair, face lines and freckles. Her white skin looks good in that colour top. No one would guess the amount of fizzy wine she drinks. Even though she is old and sad and cross, she is beautiful. And her turnout always puts me to shame.

Nan looks at my hair, my face and my scruffy school uniform. I'm not up to her scratch. Then she drops the thought and smiles at Chloë. "Hello, darling," Nan says to her.

Nan takes Chloë from me, without asking – this is yet another again thing about my mornings.

Nan puts Chloë on the table, sitting herself on a chair, in front of my baby. Nan starts spooning baby rice into Chloë's mouth, holding her sitting, with only one hand. I don't like Chloë being perched up there. I wonder, is the rice too hot still? Chloë is wincing, when it goes in, but Nan doesn't notice.

I get my own cereal. Like always now, since the day we came home from the hospital with Chloë - when Nan said, "You'll have to grow up quick, Missie. You're an adult after this."

In the kitchen, Nan is looking at me, assessing me, before saying, "Saw your mum yesterday."

Mum makes the cereal stick in my throat. I push my bowl away, trying to send the thought of Mum away too. Nan's not happy:

"Make sure you clear that up."

Nan watches me, while I scrape and rinse my bowl. "Come to the salon on Saturday and get your hair done?" Nan asks.

I would like to sort my hair out. I would like to see Marcia and the others that work there. "What time?" I ask back.

"I'll book you in, around the same time as your mum," Nan says.

No way.

"I'm busy," I say.

Nan tuts. She shakes her head. Nan doesn't see Mum the same way I do. I'd rather have messy hair, than go to the salon when Mum is there.

Nan lifts Chloë up and starts putting her coat on. I sit there. I don't have the energy to fight Nan for the right to dress my own baby -

that talk of Mum has drained me.

I watch Nan wrestle with the buggy. The lines on Nan's face crinkle deeper, as she gets more cross, with making such an effort so early in her day. Only a few minutes ago, Chloë and me were alone, singing Wheels on the Bus and "Mamamamamamumumum." I wish we were back there now.

"You going to sit there and watch all morning?" Nan is pulling the buggy backwards down the hall, getting us ready to go. Her eyes flick up to my hair again and Nan says what she wanted to say all along:

"We're getting that done Saturday, end of."

Guess I'm seeing Mum, then. Like it, or not.

Nan is strapping Chloë in. I'm trying to reach across to the hooks and get my coat. "Missie, move will you," Nan says, taking the brakes off the buggy. Chloë watches us, eyes like big questions. I wish I could push Chloë's buggy, take the handles myself, but Nan never lets me near.

As we leave, Nan stops and kisses a finger onto the photos of Mum on the hallway wall. Blasts from Mum's past.

One school photo of Mum - when she was about the age I am now - when she was just so beautiful.

One of Mum and me - a tiny photo, that looks like it's got a piece missing. Mum is holding me, on the day I am born.

One with him in as well, from about ten years ago. In that photo, Mum is on one of many holidays she took without me, when they were first together and he had more money.

She's all caramel-skin-gone-darker-in-the-sun. He's all pasty skin that's gone red in the sun, with a peeling nose.

He has an arm round her, but in a grip that looks more like control than love. Mum is smiling at the camera, but I think she looks scared. The difference between that and her school photo - it's like the shine is rubbing off her. He looks totally pleased, knows he's hooked Mum in nicely.

Back to reality and my friends are waiting for me, at the end of the passage next to Nan's house.

Derren with rucksack low, mouth popping out sounds I can't yet hear - I know he will be beatboxing, making rhythms with his voice.

Shannon is leaning, one foot up against the passage wall. She's got more new shoes – shiny black patents. Socks – wrinkled to perfection. Skirt - short. Hair - half-up, half-down, all shiny. Full face of perfect make-up. I know she'll be smelling good, of some new perfume, too. Shannon has all the toiletries.

Tommy is on the other side of the passageway. Hair floppy. Pale, spotty face. Blazer getting small. Whole, tall body directly opposite Shannon. Like always now, facing wherever Shannon is.

Derren pulls a face for Chloë, as Nan passes him. Derren knows how to make kids smile. He's got a happy home, full of nephews and nieces, where you can always hear some kind of music.

Nan doesn't slow down, or say hello to anyone. It's the same every day. She wheels past them, the heels of her boots tapping on the pavement.

I'm embarrassed. To distract myself, I listen to the beat:

"Tip, tap, buggy wheel squeak."

Shannon pushes off the wall with her foot. She waves to me. Tommy watches Shannon, gooey-eyed. Shannon pretends she doesn't notice Tommy is looking at her.

I nod hello to them all and then catch up to Nan and Chloë. Every day, I wonder - might they laugh, or leave? How could they want to hang around me? With the Baby Girl. But every morning, they drop in and follow behind.

I listen to Nan's boots and the rhythm leads me to think up a song:

> *"Tip, tap, buggy wheel squeak,*
> *Cracks in pavement rise,*
> *Nan's on a mission,*
> *Looking at me with,*
> *Grumpy, wrinkled eyes."*

My blazer pocket buzzes. I hear my friends' phones all buzz and ping behind me.

> SHANNON: What's with your Nan every day?

I shrug, in real life, so Shannon can see me ahead of her. Everyone's phones buzz again.

> SHANNON: Ha - life

Derren makes a classic phone alarm sound, with his voice. Nan looks over her shoulder at him. He stops. Buzz, ping - go the phones in the group. Derren has shared a sound file.

I press play without thinking. My phone is on loud - after Wheels on the Bus this morning. The sound file blares out. Derren has recorded himself making the alarm sound and sent it to us all. Tommy and Shannon's phones play the alarm too. It's an alarm sound clash.

Chloë pulls herself round in her buggy, trying to twist and see what's happening. This makes Nan mad, for some reason. "Stop mucking about," Nan says, straight at me, even though it's not my fault.

Then she tries to make Chloë face forward. My eyes sting, fighting back tears. The way Nan speaks to me. The way she takes over with Chloë. I need my friends not to be here, in case I can't blink these tears away.

I message them.

MISSIE: Bye

Derren bleeps like an H.G.V. He speaks like a machine, "Caution, this vehicle is reversing."

My three friends drop back and head to school the quick way, without me.

"That's better," Nan says, when they've gone. My phone buzzes again.

SHANNON: Love u x

At the drop-off, Nan takes over, again, handing Chloë to her keyworker, before I can say a proper goodbye. Nan bustles me out the door and then she just walks away, heading back to her house.

"Bye then, Nan," I whisper to myself, watching her go. I walk to school. Slowly. Alone. I keep my head down, hoping I won't be spotted, won't be shouted at.

"Baby Girl!" Someone yells at me, as I approach the school gates.

The school bell is ringing and Shannon is waiting. She always waits - and then she always links me. Ever since Chloë, Shannon links me like I might run off and away.

I smell Shannon's perfume and the lotion on her moisturised, light brown skin. She shines, where I crack and peel. I'm a yellow-grey washout, next to her.

"Baby Girl!" Some boy calls, as he runs across the yard, to reach the school doors first.

"Idiot!" Shannon shouts after him. I want to stop. I want to leave. Shannon links me tighter. She sweeps me along with her and we are, again, the last through the doors, before Latecomers kicks in.

The school prison gates slam shut behind us. "Late again, Missie," the teacher on duty says.

"We're not late," Shannon says, linking me, guiding me, down the corridor.

"We're right on time."

Shannon gets away with it - the cheekiness, the answering back. I would be in isolation for a week, if I said that to a teacher these days.

We walk to form and I breathe deep, as I do daily. Again, it's a battle. A struggle. Survival.

Shannon puts her hand on our form room door. "Ready?" She asks me.

I nod, even though I'm not ready. I'm never ready, since Chloë, for a day of school.

But then I feel Shannon linked to me, her strength pulling me through to form room. I remember her message.

SHANNON: Love u x

Love you back, Shannon. How would I get through the school day without you?

CHAPTER 2

Another day of my life at school done.

Boys shout:

"Baby Girl!"

I disappoint teachers, noting their sighs, eye rolls and impatience. I drift off in lessons, hand in half-finished homework, slip further and further behind.

I wait after the bell, until the main crowd has left school. They pour out loudly through the big gates, being normal teenagers. Shannon goes straight to dance, or sports, every day. Tommy and Derren usually drift off somewhere with the lads. I walk alone to The Lowdown, to get Chloë from nursery. With school behind me, and Chloë waiting ahead of me, it's my favourite part of the day.

At nursery, Chloë is placed into my arms. I sit her on my hip and secretly, quickly, sniff her - breathing in the air near the top of her head. She smells different after her days here. She's Chloë, plus toast, other people's hugs and a whiff of nappies.

We wheel along. I love pushing the buggy, without Nan bustling in to do it. The bit between nursery and Nan's house, Baby Girl and her baby girl in the world together. Chloë's feet bounce up and down beneath me, as we roll.

I watch the bounce-bounce, bounce-bounce.

I allow the pace of the wheels of the buggy to flow into my whole body. A low, humming beat. In my mind, I pull up Chloë's playlist and tap on a nursery rhyme that I know she likes. One that suits this buggy-wheeling moment:

> *"We're all going to the zoo tomorrow,*
> *Fix-up, day trip, straight out of here*
> *tomorrow,*
> *Big shiny bus will pick us up tomorrow,*
> *We can stay all day."*

Chloë is gooing and gaaing along with me. I don't want this to end. We're not ready to go back to Nan's - to her quiz shows and afternoon sadness. Lights are on at the library. We could go there for a while? Read a story – Chloë loves that.

I wheel us over and continue the song:

"We're going to the zoo, zoo, zoo..."

A woman stops, right in front of us, in the doorway. She's a shadow in the dark afternoon, blotted out by the lights from the library behind her.

She speaks:

"Missie?"

How does she know me?

My eyes adjust and I start to see the woman a little bit. She's a mix of something, like me. Brown skin. A high, textured ponytail. She speaks again, "Nice song."

She heard me singing? Did she hear the MC part too? She's really looking at me, so I feel like I can really look at her.

The woman's got freckles. Gold earrings. White sweats and chunky grey boots. She is smiling at me. But, I don't get it - how does she know me? How does she know my name?

She puts out a hand. What for? I don't know. I just look at it.

"I'm Gail," she says. She waits, then drops her hand. I get that feeling that I get so often, like this is just too much and I don't know what else I can do. So I shrug. Like it's nothing. Like I don't care. I do care – what I really want to do, is ask her a question:

"How do you know me?"

"Come," Gail says and shoves a flyer in my hand. Then she leaves quickly, her ponytail bouncing. I move into the library, holding the flyer, parking Chloë's buggy in the baby area.

Everyone watches us, as we get settled. I've learned, from other times like this, that the normal, older parents will be wondering if I'm Chloë's sister. I take Chloë out and let her roll and play on the soft playmat. Then I look at the flyer:

Hold the Mic.
Learn to MC.
Tuesdays 7pm at The Lowdown.
With Gail Force.

Gail Force? Is that her? She's a musician? She's an MC? And she knows who I am?

I start to wonder, could I go? Could I step back in time? To when I was a normal teenager? To the summer of last year? Shannon and me, we would meet Derren and Tommy in the park - I would MC, Derren would beatbox, Shannon would dance.

Tommy would watch – except, last year, he would watch me, not Shannon.

That's behind me now, so I push the

memory away. Chloë needs looking after.

She's got hold of a board book that's clearly been chewed and slavvered on for years. I grab it from her - I don't want her getting some other baby's germs. Chloë cries out. I feel heads turn to look at me. Chloë moves and I get a whiff of a bad nappy. That means she's going to howl in about a minute.

Why did I think it was a good idea to come in here? Why did I think Hold the Mic was a possibility for me? I should stay in the dark at Nan's, where no one watches me being an abnormal teenager. Being Baby Girl.

I wrestle a loudly miserable Chloë into her buggy, everyone just outright staring at us now. I keep my eyes on the floor and my head down, as I wheel us out of the library.

When we get home, Nan throws open her front door, before I can unlock it. "Where've you been?" She says, angrily. She's got her sweet-wine-in-the-afternoon-breath on again. I don't know how to answer. I want to shrug, but I don't want a mouthful, or a clip round the ear, so I just keep quiet.

Nan's made dinner - Shepherd's pie - but it's gone cold, because Chloë and me are late. Nan doesn't heat mine back up, but she warms Chloë's baby food and feeds her, without asking me if I want to do it. I watch Chloë enjoy her meal. Meanwhile, I'm trying to swallow mouthfuls of lumpy mash and cold mince. It sticks in my throat and I don't eat much.

Then it's bath time. I do that bit – Nan can't kneel and she doesn't like getting wet. I take special care washing Chloë every night. Rinsing her. She smiles at me. I lean over the bath and quietly sing:

"We're all going to the zoo tomorrow..."

It reminds me of that woman - Gail - and her flyer:

Hold the Mic.

After Nan says night-night to Chloë, but not me, I put the baby in her travel cot and crouch beside it. I stretch my arm into the cot, to stroke Chloë's hair. As I soothe Chloë to sleep, the quiet and the dark brings the question from tonight back to me:

How does she know me?

That woman - Gail Force.

Chloë becomes quiet and still. She looks at me with big eyes, lying on her back. She is waiting, for her lullaby. I sit on the carpet next to her cot and pull up her playlist on my phone. I sing along to her bedtime track:

"Five little ducks went swimming one day."

The ducks swim over the hill and far away. Mother Duck quack, quack, quacks. The ducks swim back. By then, Chloë is asleep.

I let my head rest, lower it to the carpet, right next to my little duck's bed. I'm so close, I can see the slow breath of Chloë sleeping.

My phone flashes beside me. It's Shannon. She's sent a picture of the Hold the Mic flyer and a message:

SHANNON: Wanna go?

Ah, Shannon. Always trying. Always reaching, to bring me back, to a normal teenager life I can no longer live in. I would love to hold a real mic in my hand. To let these words and songs out of me. But that's not my path now.

I let the lids of my eyes close, the phone screen burning bright next to me.

The Hold the Mic flyer picture is shining in the dark.

CHAPTER 3

Saturday.

Salonday.

I wheel Chloë to the salon. Marcia opens the door, when she sees us coming – ting!

Marcia hugs me and makes a fuss of Chloë too – Chloë loves it.

I miss it here. I look over at the Saturday girl they've got now – it used to be me sweeping, tidying, rinsing out sinks. I'd get £15 cash in my hand. It was a slice of freedom.

But look at me now. Standing here, feeling far away from myself, as I watch Marcia talk to Chloë, bending down to make her smile in her buggy seat.

Nan is blowdrying a customer's hair. I can tell from how Nan is not looking over, that she knows we are here. Why doesn't she acknowledge us? Nan is often like that.

Marcia walks to her chair and swings it round, inviting me over to sit. I wheel Chloë towards Marcia. "Are you doing my hair today?" I ask, hoping.

"Yes, my love," Marcia smiles. I unwind – I'm less stressed, now I know it's Marcia. That means no Nan yanking my hair in a grump, pulling my head around, like she normally does.

Marcia parks Chloë, so Chloë can see me in the chair, then carries on speaking, as she starts work. "Your nan is seeing to your mum's hair," Marcia says.

I feel my hands tighten on the armrests, as Marcia places a gown over me. Mum. Already. Always Mum - and always Nan, jumping to Mum's beat.

I take my bobble out and stare at my reflection - I'm all dark circles and yellow-grey skin. I can't stand to see my face and neck sticking out of the gown, looking at a ghost of who I was. I watch the new Saturday girl in the mirror, sweeping up behind me - the normal teenager I used to be.

There's a Hold the Mic poster, stuck to the mirror near Marcia's chair. There's a stack of Hold the Mic flyers, on the shelf under the mirror.

Seeing those words - "Hold the Mic" -

reminds me that I never replied to Shannon's message, about going there. She didn't ask me about it later either. No reply is a reply, I guess.

I move my gaze away from the poster, the flyers, the idea of Hold the Mic – it's a dream and I have to live in my reality.

Marcia stands behind me. Her dark skin glows with daily moisturisation. Her cherry-coloured lip sheen pops. She is wearing a bright patterned dress – white and green. I feel like I don't belong next to someone so welcoming, so shining. I want to slide down the seat, on to the floor, out of the door and away.

I get my hair washed by Saturday Girl and then sit again, at Marcia's chair. Chloë squawks, entertained by all the movement and noises. Marcia talks to me, while she works, as if I am a normal, everyday person:

"How's school?"

"How's the baby getting on?"

I'm lost for answers.

"Hard to say, right?" Marcia says, as she smiles at me in the mirror.

I feel so ashamed - for being rude, for being silent. I can feel hot tears coming. I don't want to cry here, in front of everyone. I close my eyes, hoping that will help to stop my sadness. I focus my mind on the sounds of the salon, instead of thinking about how I'm feeling.

Scissors snipping. Customer chatter. Hair wash, till ding, doorbell ring, hairdryer. It all blends together, a track I could write lyrics to.

This is helping, so I stay with it. I pick one of Chloë's nursery rhymes - Oh Dear, What Can the Matter Be. I mix the melody, the words, the salon sounds. I call the song Saturday, Salon Day:

> *"Oh dear, how come it's Saturday,*
> *Weeks slipping by,*
> *From my life,*
> *I'm so far you see,*
> *Used to have fun,*
> *Chatting some,*
> *Earning money,*
> *Free,*
> *Now I don't feel like I'm here."*

I think I can ride this out, stay in Marcia's chair, get my hair done, not try to run, or shrug. Act normal. I listen to the sounds some more. Can I think up a second verse?

And then, ting. The door opens, in a particular way. I know it will be him. I feel Marcia stop working and breathe in. Let me get this over and look.

There they are. Mum and him.

The door's wide, letting the cold in. Mum's standing just inside the salon, shrunk into herself, hands in her pockets. He's big and filling the rest of the space, arms wide, chest up.

Mum's wearing a faded, black tracksuit. Her hair is pulled through the snapback of one of his old caps, which is too big for her head. She's spotty and thin. She's a no-brand, worn-out version of that woman I met the other night, Gail Force.

He slaps Mum's behind - it makes her jump. She squeaks and looks embarrassed, but reassembles her face quickly, giggles and pretends she likes being treated like that, in front of us all. I think of the song I was just writing, how Mum always pretends:

"No, here, nothing the matter be."

Nan bustles over, ducking round him, to give Mum a hug, which she doesn't give back.

"Make her look beautiful," he says to Nan.

"She always looks beautiful," Marcia replies, cutting my hair, not looking at him, as she speaks.

"No one asked you," he says to Marcia, before adding, sarcastically, "*Mum*."

"Come on, darling," Nan says to Mum,

leading Mum to her salon chair.

I catch his eye by accident. Oh no. I drop my look down quickly, but it's too late. "And you can keep your mouth shut as well," he says, slowly, his voice deep. I want him to leave, to leave us all alone.

"You hear me?" He growls at me.

I nod, then stare at the floor.

"I'll be back in an hour," he says. He leaves the door wide open behind him, to show he's the boss.

Marcia finishes my hair, but her smile's gone. I know how she feels - that pig in her life and she can't be rid of him.

Mum sits in Nan's salon chair. Biting her nails, swiping through her phone, tapping her leg up and down. Nan tries to talk to Mum, like Mum's a normal person. When Mum looks up and grunts an answer, I catch a look at her reflection. She's still got a beautiful face, under all that thin tiredness, under everything he does to her and she does to herself.

I watch Mum spot a Hold the Mic flyer, near Nan's salon chair. She picks it up, reads it, her face twisting. Then she waves the flyer in the mirror and barks at Nan:

"What are these, Mum?"

"I don't know, darling," Nan says, in a fake voice that sounds way too high and sweet to be true.

"How long has she been back?" Mum demands. Marcia has stopped doing my hair and is watching the scene at Nan's chair as well now.

"I don't know, Belle sweetheart," Nan says. Nan is trying to comb out Mum's hair, but Mum jerks away from her. Mum picks up the whole stack of flyers that are nearest to her. I realise the flyers are everywhere in the salon.

"These need chucking," Mum raises her voice at Nan and now everyone's looking. Saturday Girl has stopped sweeping up. Mum points at the piles of flyers about the place. "All of them."

Marcia walks tall, across the salon. She takes the flyers from Mum's hand. "I'll keep them by *my* chair in *my* salon," Marcia says, then returns to her chair, puts the flyers down and continues working on my hair.

"You can keep them in the bin," Mum says, angrily. Mum sits back in her chair and shakes her head, like she just can't believe it. "What has she come back for?" Mum says to Nan. Marcia answers Mum in a cool, calm voice:

"Gail has the same right to be here that you do. She grew up here as well."

Mum raises an eyebrow and looks at

Marcia in the mirror.

"You'll know all about it, when Kyren finds out, Marcia," Mum says.

"So be it," Marcia replies.

I'm watching, thinking that these Hold the Mic flyers have got Mum so tightly wound. Mum notices and spits a question at me:

"Do you want a picture?"

I look away. I watch Marcia stack the flyers she took from Mum. This Hold the Mic thing is causing all kinds of drama. But who is Gail Force? Why does she know me? Why does Mum know her? And him? And Marcia?

Everything continues, like we've pressed play again. Marcia finishes up my hair. I look new – me, but not me. Marcia won't take money from Nan for my hair. She kisses me on both cheeks and gives Chloë five pounds pocket money. "Buy her some sweets," Marcia says.

"She's too little," I say.

"Well, buy yourself some, then," Marcia folds my hand over the five-pound note and winks at me. Mum is deep in her phone and Nan is back quietly working on Mum's hair. Neither of them look over, as I get ready to go with Chloë.

I check the Hold the Mic poster in the mirror one last time, before we leave. I know that no one will tell me anything – they never do.

Which means, if I want to know what the issue is with Gail Force, I'll need to go to Hold the Mic find out.

CHAPTER 4

My phone ping, ping, pings.

SHANNON:	Tuesday!
SHANNON:	*typing…*
SHANNON:	HOLD THE MIC NIGHT
SHANNON:	You there, Misdemeanour?

I picture Shannon - tonging and teasing, spraying her hair. Plumping and glossing her lips. Looking through her clothes. Messaging. Humming and dancing - always dancing. Being a normal teenager.

I turn my phone over, screen down. I'm sitting on my bed. Wearing my saggy, black leggings, my tired, denim jacket. Plain t-shirt that's gone not-white, from too much washing. Everything too tight, or too short, or too faded.

Why did I ever say I would attend Hold the Mic?

Who cares why Mum wasn't happy about those flyers? Who cares about being an MC? I'm not shaming myself any more than I already do at school. Going out into the normal teenager world at night too? Looking like this? At least, in the day, I have my school uniform on. But my night-time clothes show me up, for the real state of my life.

I can't do it. I pick up my phone again – ready to send that sorry guys, gotta bail message.

TOMMY:	*typing…*
DERREN:	Legends of the scene incoming
TOMMY:	*typing…*
SHANNON:	Let's do this

I feel like this situation is sliding out of my control. They're going to be here, before I know it. And then I will have to tell them face-to-face that I'm not going to Hold the Mic.

I start to tap on my screen, to compose a message. Meanwhile, Shannon is sending all kinds of mic and music emojis, while I plod slowly on my keyboard, trying to get my own message together.

And then a rhythmical bang, buh, bang, bang on Nan's front door. Oh no - that's Derren – I know the rhythm of his door knock. I hear Nan answer the front door, all friendly – because she's had just enough wine to make her happy:

"Come in, darlings."

Do my friends notice how differently Nan acts - from when she's had no wine, to when she has? I hear chatter, coming from down the hall. Derren's quick pace conversation. Shannon's sweet, chitchat tone. If Nan knew where we were going, she wouldn't be so keen to talk to them all, I bet.

Knock, knock – goes my bedroom door. It's Shannon, I know. I wish I could hide under the bed, or something, like I was little. Shannon and me used to play hide-and-seek all the time, back when we were kids.

"Coming, ready or not?" Shannon calls through the door, like we're small again.

"I'm not playing," I say back, my voice wobbling - I sound like a little kid too. I wish I was one. I wish I wasn't what I am now - an abnormal teenager, who has to be a grown-up.

The bedroom door opens. Shannon peeps through, the light from Nan's hallway falls in a long, thin triangle upon the spare bedroom carpet.

I turn away. It won't work. I know Shannon won't let me ignore her, but I wish just turning away was enough to make me invisible. To get Shannon to leave me alone.

I hear the door gently click shut. Shannon is standing in the room now. I turn to look at her. Even though it is dark, Shannon still shines. Tonight, she is wearing a blush pink, furry jacket, with brightly coloured pom pom earrings and shimmering, multi-coloured leggings.

Shannon has contoured her face some and popped a bright pink lip on. She looks like the grown-up one, not me. She is the one who has her look, and her life, together. She stands tall, straight, dancer's stance. I'm slumped on Nan's spare clickety, rickety bed. I wish I could be like her.

Shannon's voice is kind and soft, as she says, "Your hair looks so good, you know." Shannon, you sweetheart - she's told me this ten times already, since yesterday.

Since I decided on Saturday, that I was going to go out to Hold the Mic tonight, I've had beats and bars and rhythms running through my mind non-stop. I've been picturing The Lowdown at night, when it's not Chloë's nursery – when it's a place for normal teenagers. I've been telling myself, I might dare hold the actual mic and say some of my lyrics into it.

I've been hoping I can also learn something about Mum - something that means I don't have to feel afraid of her, and him, all the time. They always have all the power and don't they know it? I want something they don't know I have.

Marcia's salon comes back to me. Those flyers for Hold the Mic. Mum in a flap, me wondering what had got her so raged. Am I really going to pass on the chance to find out more about this Gail woman, just because I can't be a sharp goddess like Shannon?

"Shall I help you get ready?" Shannon asks.

I am ready, I think. But I'm too embarrassed to say that. Shannon knows things I don't. Maybe she can make it all better, by putting some lipstick on me...

"Here," Shannon pulls off her shiny and new, black trainers. She picks up my old pumps from near the chest of drawers.

"These go with my outfit better," Shannon says. "Do you mind if I borrow them?"

I'm so grateful to this girl, but can't show

it, so I shrug.

Next, Shannon passes me a hoodie she has tied round her waist. The hoodie's mostly black, with a bright pink hood lining. "Put it on under your jacket," Shannon says. "I reckon it will look really good on you."

I pop the denim jacket back on over the hoodie, look down at my feet, in Shannon's new trainers. I can live with this ensemble. I'm a fake and a borrower, but I don't want to feel like Hold the Mic tonight was another thing I can't do – like homework and hanging out with friends and giving Chloë her breakfast, instead of Nan taking over. And I want to know more about Gail.

"Let's do it," I say, trying to sound like I mean it. Shannon links me and I feel myself relax. We leave the bedroom for the naked, overhead bulb light of Nan's hallway.

Nan's laughing with the boys and ignoring Chloë, who is trying to pull herself up to standing, by holding on to Nan's tights. Chloë slips down, unable to get a good grip – Nan doesn't even notice that Chloë has plonked on her bottom and looks sad about it.

I swoop down and pick Chloë up. Why am I the only one who ever seems to see what Chloë needs, when she needs it? Drool drops from Chloë's mouth, landing on my denim jacket. I wipe it away, hoping no one clocked it.

"Shall I put her down first, Nan?" I ask, trying to get Nan's attention. Nan looks at the boys and rolls her eyes, as she answers me:

"I've looked after babies before, you know?"

Nan is swaying slightly, in her slippers. Can the others tell? Do they know Nan has been steadily drinking sweet, fizzy wine, since she got home from work, earlier this afternoon?

Chloë pulls at my chin, marking the skin on my face with her little, grasping fingertips. Yes, I think, I will stay with Chloë, where I belong. I'm not leaving Chloë alone, with only Nan's glazed eyes to look into. I don't feel right about it.

Nan grabs the baby from me, actually hurting me a bit, as Chloë is wrenched from my arms. "Go on. Go out, darling," Nan says, then she presses a fiver in my hand quickly.

It's times like this, I feel ashamed for thinking bad of Nan, for not telling her I am going to Hold the Mic. She can be kind and generous.

Everyone's looking at me, even Chloë. Waiting. "You going then?" Nan's got one hand on the front door, to open it.

Wait, I want to say. Let me hug my baby. Give her a proper night-night. Nan's got a tight hold of Chloë, though, and the door out to the evening, to the way to Hold the Mic, is now open. My friends are filing out. Shannon links me again and moves me out into the dark with her.

The door to Nan's closes shut and I stand on the path, not moving, while Derren and Tommy chat on and walk ahead. I see the shadow of Nan, through the glass of her front door. Chloë is jiggling up and down, in Nan's arms.

Above us, it's a clear and bright night. I imagine stars shining, though I can't see any.

I think of bedtime. Chloë will wait for me to come and sing to her, in her travel cot:

> *"Twinkle, twinkle, little star,*
> *Chloë will wonder where you are,*
> *Nan will put her down, say bye,*
> *Nan won't sing about the sky,*
> *Nan won't sing about the stars,*
> *Chloë will wonder where you are."*

CHAPTER 5

The Lowdown is a different place at night, when the teenagers take over.

Lads block the path to the door, with their bikes and hoods. The smell of weed clings to them. I slow down. So do Tommy and Shannon. But Derren speeds up, gliding ahead, into the group huddle. He makes a beatbox sound - fist-bump, hand-slap, shoulder-touch. They part and we walk in.

Someone calls, "Baby Girl!" Someone else barks like a dog. Derren holds the door open for us, like this is all part of the fun. We're in, through, that part over.

There's no playmats or baby toys now, like when it's nursery. The ceiling overhead lights are off. A panel of disco lights flash instead, slow sequence, on a chair, next to a portable speaker. And there it stands, the lights sequencing around it, the mic.

Close by, a table – on it, a laptop and CDJs. Headphones.

People mill around the edges of the room. A guy in a boxfresh snapback, trackie top and loose jeans walks out and starts working the CDJs, listening, one can handheld to his ear. He nods and a bass beat rolls out from the speaker. People stand up, come a little closer.

Then she is here. The woman with the flyers, from outside the library. The woman who got Mum in a fluster and Nan speaking in her high-pitched, I'm-not-lying, lying voice.

Gail Force.

She's wearing a gold, tight-fit bomber jacket. It sets her brown-blonde curls shining and her hoops glistening. She's got a black text on white fabric, Just Do It t-shirt and white leggings. She's wearing white and gold hi-tops.

She takes the mic, nods to the DJ and jumps on the beat:

> "Gail Force,
> Full throttle to the floor,

Leave em wanting more,
Don't hold back,
Full mic attack,
Went to The States and learned,
And now I will put back."

Garage MC style – like the music Mum listened to, when I was a kid. I'm watching something I've already seen, even though I haven't. I know how Gail Force is going to sound, what her flows will be like. I know them in my blood.

When I focus back in on Hold the Mic, I see people are full of whoops and cheers. Gail is standing still, her face wearing a little grin. She winks at us all and does a tiny bow. What must it be like? To feel so confident? With everyone's eyes on you? I can't picture that ever being me.

Gail motions to the chairs that are in a horseshoe shape around her. People sit, except me. I stand, rooted. I know I'm staring, but I can't snap myself out of it.

Shannon nudges me and we get the last chairs, close to the left side of Gail Force.

Once everyone's sitting, Gail sits too and waits for us all to settle. She's still and calm and pretty soon everyone else is too, when they realise she is waiting. This room is hers and, because everyone else is looking only at Gail, it feels safe for me to take a good look at her too.

She seems so the opposite of rinsed-out, no-effort-in-herself Mum. I wonder, how they can know each other? They don't seem like they belong on the same planet.

I still want to ask Gail that question – the one I've kept thinking, on and off, ever since that evening outside the library:

"How do you know me?"

And now, also, what about:

"How do you know Mum?"

But then, urgh. Gail is so special - look at how everyone wants to be near her, even though they've only just met her, a few minutes ago. Placing Gail next to Mum in my thoughts feels all kinds of wrong.

I realise my face is scrunched up, as if there is a bad smell under my nose, when Gail catches my eye. "Everything okay, Missie?" Gail asks.

The heads in a horseshoe shape all snap in my direction. I've never had so many people look at me. I need to get their attention off me fast. I nod quickly and stare down at the floor. I think only about tonight and being here. Empty my head of all the questions, the memory of the scene with Mum getting irate about Gail's flyers. Act empty, like I've learned to.

"Right then," Gail speaks. Everyone turns to look back her. I raise my own head, once I sense I'm no longer the object of anyone's focus. Gail is holding out the mic. The DJ has stepped up the tempo and intensity of the beats and the lights are flashing in synch.

"Who's first?" Gail says. No one moves. Some people look at the mic, some at each other, egging each other on. Some look at the floor. Gail is holding out the mic like it's an offer, an invitation. I wish I dared to get up and go for it. I can't imagine a nicer person to take a mic from, than Gail.

But I am captured, weighted, in this chair. I live with heavy air all around me and tonight that air feels like chains, holding me, keeping me seated.

"Just your names," Gail says to the room. People move, relax. Gail watches them – and I watch her. "That's all you need to do tonight," Gail continues. She stands, holding the mic in two hands, close to her mouth. She speaks to us all:

"The mic is your friend. It's there for you. It wants to hear you. Just tell the mic your MC name. Make it up tonight and change it tomorrow. It doesn't matter."

Gail catches my eye briefly, as she says this next part:

"Everyone needs to say at least one thing into the mic tonight. You'll all feel better when you do. Tonight is just about getting started."

I feel a movement nearby. Derren is up. He does a little dip, as he approaches Gail and holds out his hand for the mic. Gail nods, smiles and passes the mic to him.

Derren holds his hand at the top of the mic, tipping the bottom of it high in the air, so it's on a diagonal slope down to his mouth. It's a classic MC style – and this will not be the first time Derren's held, or used, a mic.

He's grown up around music. It fills his house. It's what half his family do, for at least part of their living, and for all their fun. Derren is inherited into the scene. It's just in him.

Derren beatboxes the sound of vinyl scratching, then the wind-down of a record. The

DJ stops the real beat for a minute too.

"D-Damager," Derren announces and hands the mic back. Gail gives him a fist bump. The DJ spins the beat back up and we're off again.

People get up. No one's as good as Derren. Some people have average MC names, most suck. When my lot get up, I worry for them, but they're okay. Tommy just says, "Tommy T," with his hair hanging down over his face, hiding.

Shannon says, "Shanny." Not in a shy way, just I am who I am.

When she comes to sit back down, she nudges me, grinning, pointing at the mic, meaning I should get up there and hold it too.

But even though I spend all the time I can, performing in my mind, or for Chloë, I feel like I don't belong here. I feel like everyone, all the normal teenagers, they are here for a laugh and to be curious and I'm here because this woman knows my name and Mum hates her and I want to know why. They can come here and be free, but I am here with all the layers of my life around me still. And those layers hold me back, like they've always done.

There is only me left. Gail Force is holding out the mic to me – her eyebrows asking the question, "You going to do this?"

I think of what brought me here – all my questions. And what I will be going back to – my same-every-day life. What if I never get a mic offered to me again? What if this is my only chance?

I think of Chloë. I picture her, fanging the travel cot, as I'm whispering fast-spit lyrics to her at bedtime. Chloë is my answer. I fix her in my mind. I stay sitting - my legs are shaking too much, for me to dare stand up.

"What's your MC name?" Gail says, looking right at me, with shining, kind eyes. And then she just sort of puts the mic in my hand, as if I can't say no.

The mic nearly slips through my sweaty palms. I hold it awkwardly. It's way heavier than I imagined.

All the room's eyes are upon me. It makes me feel like I do, when the shadows at the edges of Nan's spare room creep towards me at night.

I can't picture Chloë now. MC name? Who am I kidding? I'm not so brave I dare claim an MC name. I'm not even brave enough to say I don't want to say anything. So, even though, I don't want to, I speak my everyday name into the mic:

"Missie."

That's it. That's all I manage. Now, please get this microphone away from me.

Gail leans out to fist-bump me. My hand, is shaking. The skin of my knuckles makes brief contact with Gail's. I drop the mic into her hand.

I feel like a failure for the rest of the night.

Everyone else is switched on to Gail and to each other – the energy of speaking into the mic has linked them all, where I just feel even further apart from these normal teenagers.

Gail talks to the room about her life in America. How she worked as a music producer and mentor for kids. How she used to be a garage MC in the UK, years ago.

Gail describes how to jump on a beat, but I'm not able to pay attention. Some people have a go, looking like amateurs next to Gail, though she never makes them feel like they are.

Gail plays different beats and talks about

flows and finding your own MC style. She knows so much. Everyone is listening, except me. Her words are just flowing past me, like traffic on a busy street.

I stare at Gail. Her face looks so familiar to me. From the side. From the front. From all ways. I wish I knew the answer to my question:

"How do you know me?"

While Gail continues and the session rolls on, the question loops and loops in my mind. I decide to set it to a beat, to try and control the inner repetition. I take the bass I can hear from the speaker and mentally blend it with one of Chloë's favourites - Baa Baa Black Sheep:

> *"How do you know me?*
> *How do you know my name?*
> *My mum knows you too,*
> *But you are not the same.*
>
> *You are a master,*
> *She is so lame,*
> *I feel stupid sitting here,*
> *Why did I say my name?"*

I keep working on the track, switching up flows, experimenting on it, in the mixing desk of my mind. It gets me through, until the end of the session.

The DJ is packing up. Gail is moving everyone out through the doors, telling them, "See you next week." And I am no closer to knowing anything about her. Why did I come here and spend time in a place I don't belong and make everything feel worse to me than it already does?

Shannon, Derren and Tommy have stood up and are waiting for me. Normal teenagers. Shannon grins and links me, saying, "Wasn't that brilliant?"

"Quality flows," Derren says. Tommy nods.

We move to the door, which Gail is holding open for us. I'm already out of time. I'm no nearer knowing anything. I bet I never will.

"Goodnight, everyone," Gail says. Then, as I pass her, she speaks only to me - it feels like it's on purpose:

"Goodnight, Missie."

As we walk home. Derren beatboxes all

the way, while Shannon pulls me close and whispers, "Gail Force likes you."

"What do you mean?" I ask. Does Shannon know something about Gail Force that I can learn? Shannon's mum and mine are the same age, so maybe Shannon's mum knows Gail too?

"She remembered your name," Shannon says, almost skipping us down the pavement, her hair swinging. "She didn't remember anyone else's." Shannon is so innocent.

Gail already knows my name, Shannon – I think about saying this, but hold the words back. It feels secret and complicated and I know all about secret and complicated. I'm different enough from everyone else already.

And then, as if she can hear my thoughts, Shannon says, "You're not like the rest of us."

I don't have time to ask her what she means, we're near her house now. I pull away alone, to head down the alleyway to Nan's. The others watch me from the top, making sure I get back okay.

My feet tap along the pavement. A song begins in my mind:

"Not the like the rest of us,
Not like the rest of us."

Tip-tap, pavement beat. I reach Nan's path. I stop and wave. The beat ends. My friends go.

In the living room, Nan's spark out on the sofa. Chloë is sleeping on Nan's lap. The TV's still on.

I knew Nan wasn't going to put her properly to bed. Chloë could've woken up and been scared. She could've rolled off Nan's lap and fallen on the floor. She could've crawled away, put her finger in a plug socket, pulled the TV on herself. And all while Nan was snoring away, in a fizzy wine sleep.

If I go out again, I'm putting the baby to sleep first.

If I go out again? Get real. This is not a situation I can ignore. Chloë's needs come first.

As I lift Chloë up, I admit something to myself - Hold the Mic isn't a life for me.

I'll be here watching telly with Nan and Chloë, while my friends are out, living those normal teenager lives. I can't leave my baby girl here without me.

Once Chloë's back in her cot and covered in a blanket, I lie on the bed, fully clothed, in the dark. I'm too sad to put the covers on, to make myself warm and a bit more comfortable.

I hear the beat from my feet on the pavement again – it's on playback in my head, as I lie there:

> *"Not like the rest of us,*
> *Not like the rest of us."*

CHAPTER 6

But what Shannon says, it stays with me.

"Gail Force likes you."

Does she?

I've only met her twice and yet she's been kinder to me than anyone in my own family has ever been. Would it be so bad, if I was to find a way to keep going back to Hold the Mic and see her again? Even if I never get the guts to perform a song, at least I will be near someone who doesn't say my name like it's a swear word.

It was good to get out from under Nan's nightly feet. It was good to go to Hold the Mic, that one time. But what about Chloë? I can't leave her again, to fall asleep on Nan. I want her to have a proper bedtime.

I spend the next few days worrying about how to solve this problem, until it's the weekend.

Saturday. Nan is back late, which means she has called at the pub on her way home from work. I've got Chloë bathed and ready for bed and I'm singing my new version of Baa Baa Black Sheep, lullaby style, when I hear Nan come noisily in the door, in a trying-to-be-quiet way.

"Hello?" Nan calls. "Where are you both?" I hear more than one drink in Nan's voice. Chloë's body changes, from getting sleepy, to waking back up. She looks to the door.

I hear Nan walking down the hallway, so I scrabble up, to stop her coming in and getting Chloë excited. Nan stops at the door, not coming in. "I brought fish & chips," she says, from the hall. Chloë looks at me, I smile at her – I don't want her to notice Nan's drunk, or that I'm bothered by it.

"It's just Nan," I say to Chloë, like it's good news. I hear Nan go to the kitchen. I pick Chloë back up, she is snuggly in her sleeping bag. We go and find Nan together in the kitchen.

"Here, give her those," Nan puts a few chips on a plate for Chloë. I don't want to feed Chloë this late. She might be sick in her sleep, but I don't dare tell Nan now - I can tell by the way she's moving around, she's just the wrong side of drunk and will get quickly annoyed.

I smile at Chloë. I break up the hot chip, blowing on it, cooling it right down. Nan gives me some of her fish and a few chips. I won't turn it down - I've only had toast for dinner tonight. We eat quietly for a bit. I let Nan sort her hunger out. The words from last week drum a pattern in my head, as I watch Nan:

"Not like the rest of us."

I feel such a pull, such a need, to go back to Hold the Mic. I want to have just one piece of something for myself, which makes the next words come out:

"Can I go out again next week, Nan?"

Nan keeps eating, but in a thinking-about-it way.

"Where are you going?" Nan says, between mouthfuls. I think about how to answer - I can't lie, but I can't tell the truth either.

"To The Lowdown," I say. Nan screws her chip paper up.

"You think I don't know that's where you were before?" Nan says. I can see Nan's eyes have no sparkle – her trip to the pub has taken that away for the rest of the night. I know I have to speak nicely to try and reach her. I put a smile into my voice and ignore Nan's (correct) accusation.

"Just wondering if you'll babysit Chloë again for me?" The thought of leaving Chloë with Nan scares me so much, but I try not to let it show in the way I'm speaking.

"I can put her to bed for you first, though. I don't want to put you to any effort," I say. I hold Chloë tight to me.

Nan pours herself a glass, from a small bottle of fizzy wine she's found in the fridge. "Don't want to put me to any effort. That's a good one," Nan says, taking her drink and sitting in her armchair. Remote control in her other hand, Nan channel surfs, while she sips.

I have to know, so I ask, "Can I then, Nan?"

Nan keeps her eyes on the telly. "What do you think your mum's gonna say?"

I want to give the world's biggest shrug. Who cares what Mum says, or thinks, or does?

But this is also an opening. Nan is acknowledging that there's an issue with Gail Force. Perhaps I can find something out from Nan, while the fizzy wine makes her more likely to talk.

I sit with Chloë, on Nan's small sofa. I keep my eyes on the telly. I make my voice casual, like my next question doesn't really matter:

"Why's everyone getting so bothered by those flyers, Nan?"

"What flyers?" Nan replies, her voice getting higher.

Oh, okay. We're really pretending now.

I yawn, as if I'm too tired to be bothered to ask:

"Does Mum know Gail Force?"

"Gail *Force*," Nan says, stressing the Force part. "Silly name." Nan finishes her drink.

"I'll get you some water," I say. When I pass the water to Nan, she drinks it down, taking ages about it, like she's using the drink as an excuse not to talk.

I stand behind the kitchen worktop,

looking out at Nan - it's a rare thing, her being on the back foot with me. I pick up Nan's fizzy wine bottle and wait.

"Bring me the rest of that, will you?" Nan eventually says, without looking at me. "It won't keep 'til tomorrow."

I pour the yellow bubbles slowly into Nan's glass, stopping the flow halfway, to ask her, "Who is Gail Force, Nan?" Nan motions for me to carry on pouring. But I wait.

"Gail is Marcia's foster daughter," Nan says. "Adopted. In the end." Nan waves her hand, meaning, hurry up with that drink.

Gail and him are connected by Marcia? It feels wrong that two such different people could be tied to each other. And by Marcia, who I've known all my life.

Is Mum jealous or something? That would be just like her. She's so insecure. And she would hate Gail, just for being everything's she's not. That's how Mum's mind turns. I pour the rest of the wine into Nan's glass, while thinking about asking my question a different way.

"Is that how Mum knows Gail then?" I try asking.

Nan cuts me off, "Do you wanna watch a film?" Nan's pointing at the telly, with the remote. Her tone means this is the end of that subject – which also means it's only the beginning. I am dying to know more.

"Do you know Gail too, Nan?" I ask, trying to sound as innocent as possible, moving Chloë up my shoulder, because she's getting sleepy now.

Nan mutes the telly.

"Leave it, Missie." Nan looks at me. Her mouth is wrinkled, her eyes unsteady.

I feel more and more questions bubbling up in me, but Nan sits like a brick wall in her armchair. She's got her back fully turned to me, as she pulls the movie menu up on her TV. End of chat, I guess.

I take Chloë to the bedroom and gently place her in the cot. She is almost asleep.

I'm dying to figure things out - about him and Mum and Gail - but I don't have enough information.

Gail and him must know each other. I don't know all the timelines of him being in and out of foster care and prison and stuff, but there's obviously some kind of crossover. And

Mum has someone she doesn't want in her life, apart from me. Weirdly, that makes me feel closer to Gail, though I hardly know her - the idea, that Mum hates us both.

As I lie next to the cot, I see my phone on the floor, where I left it earlier. It's full of notifications. Full of communications from normal teenagers.

SHANNON:	Won my dancing comp!
DERREN:	Yes
SHANNON:	Who's celebrating?
DERREN:	At my uncles but join you later
SHANNON:	Missie?
TOMMY:	Yes

Man of few messages responds already.

And on and on. They arrange times and locations. Cinema. Derren seeing them after. Shannon messages me privately as well.

SHANNON:	Please come x

As if I'm leaving Nan in charge tonight. As if I'm going to go to the cinema. With

Shannon and Tommy.

No.

The bright lights of their notifications flow past me, on my phone screen. Normal teenagers reply, contribute to the chat. But what can I say? Sorry guys - got to stay in with my baby and my drunk Nan tonight.

I pull one of Chloë's nursery rhymes up, on my phone. I hold the speaker close to my ear, volume as low as possible.

I need to sing myself a lullaby tonight:

> *"Twinkle, twinkle, I can't see the stars,*
> *Cannot see a future, only staying where we are,*
> *Others will climb above this world, so high,*
> *They will shine bright, like diamonds, in the sky,*
> *They don't twinkle for us, those stars,*
> *No one wonders where we are."*

CHAPTER 7

Sunday. Nan crawls to her bed, at dawn. She wakes Chloë and me with the click of her bedroom door.

I am so tired, but, once Chloë wakes, she's awake and never goes back to sleep.

At least we have the lounge to ourselves, happy day. A shared bowl of microwave porridge for us both. Then TV and carpet rolling for the baby. Schoolwork for me. Nan will be asleep for hours.

They are singing nursery rhymes on the telly. Chloë loves it - I swear, she can recognise the tunes. She's so hyped, when she hears Twinkle, Twinkle. I bet she remembers me singing it to her.

I pick up Chloë and stand her on my lap,

facing me. I skip back to Twinkle Twinkle on the TV and MC for my number one fan:

> *"Twinkle, twinkle, you're my little star,*
> *You will be my future,*
> *I'll be where you are,*
> *I will watch you rise above this world so high,*
> *You'll be my bright diamond, bright like a diamond in the sky,*
> *Twinkle, sparkle, shining little star,*
> *I will always be wherever you are."*

Chloë grins. She pats my face and I turn her round on my lap to watch the next song. Incy Wincy. We watch that spider over and over again, climbing up and getting washed down the waterspout. I can relate.

"That's like me, doing homework," I say to Chloë and put her back down on the carpet. "Trying to scrabble back up to where I was, every day getting washed back down."

But Chloë doesn't hear me – well, she does, but she doesn't know what I mean. I sit for a bit with my Maths books, trying to puzzle it out. I used to find Maths okay, but, after I missed school when Chloë came, I slipped behind. Now the numbers swirl round on the page in front of me, every time I try to get to know them again.

I pick up my phone, to use the calculator. The screen lights up with a message, at the very second I unlock it.

> DERREN: Who wants to practise for Hold the Mic?

I wait – for Shannon, or Tommy, to reply, with a, "See you there".

But they don't. Nothing comes in on the chat.

I check their status – looks like neither of them are online. I wonder, are they together? But so what if they are, I tell myself. I put down my phone. Best to crack on with this Maths I can't do.

But the thought of some one-to-one time with Derren and his beatboxing rhythms, keeps tapping in my head, like the start of an instrumental. Plus, Derren is amazing at Maths – he's on accelerated learning. I could ask him to help me.

I pick my phone up again.

Derren's message is still sitting there unanswered. I know he won't wait long, before he goes and finds something else to do. Derren is a person of action, not a man of few words. Do I dare? Can I go out and be a normal teenager, for just a little while?

I look at Chloë. She needs some fresh air. Once Nan gets up, I'll be peeling potatoes and scrubbing veg for Sunday lunch and we'll have to stay in with Nan for the rest of the day. Shall I go now, while I still can?

I can do my homework later, watching Sunday evening TV. And when will there be another time, when Derren messages and the other two don't answer, and I'm the one who is actually free?

I pick Chloë up and hold her, to help me feel brave, as I tap out a reply.

MISSIE:	We will
DERREN:	Yes
MISSIE:	As in, me and Chloë
DERREN:	Course
DERREN:	Park in 20?

Park in 20... It's the Year 9 to 10 summer, all over again. I reply.

MISSIE: K

I feel good about this, deciding to go out. It's still morning, which means most of our year won't be out and about. And Derren's easy to be around. I feel like we will be able to just chat about music, maybe I can try out some lyrics. I even start throwing together the shape of another verse of:

> *"Twinkle, twinkle, now is where we are,*
> *Getting prepped to make new beats, write lyrics in the park,*
> *Maybe get some help with Maths, I could make a start..."*

But it takes more like double 20 minutes, to get me and Chloë out of the door – she fills her nappy, just as I am strapping her in the buggy, and I have to deal with that and calm her down, before I can get to the park.

And, when I do, I've taken so long – and been too distracted to hear the buzz of my phone. Now all three of them are there. And I forgot my Maths book, after all that nappy stress.

Derren's sitting at the top of the climbing frame. Tommy's on the swing. Shannon's sitting on Tommy's lap. I wanted it to just be Derren and me. To just be about the music. And a bit of Maths.

I think of the Incy Wincy song we watched earlier. I feel myself slide down my internal waterspout a little, just like that spider. And I hate myself for my feelings – they're all my friends, after all. Why shouldn't Shannon and Tommy be here too? I don't own this park.

Shannon hears Chloë's buggy wheels clatter across the rough park ground towards her. She stands up super quick and steps away from Tommy. She waves at us. I act blank, like I saw nothing of her sitting on Tommy's lap.

Now, I'm nearer, I can hear that they're talking about last night. Stuff I can't join in with and don't care to hear about. I say hi, then put Chloë in the baby swing, opposite them all. Hello normal teenagers. I thought I could join you, but I belong here, on the abnormal teenagers side, pushing my baby on the swing.

Dog mess, broken glass, litter. I avoid it, as I step forward and back, forward and back. Pushing Chloë, gently. I feel alone, even though I am with my baby and my friends.

I watch Chloë's little feet flap in her frilly socks. I look at the tiny yellow duck that's stitched on to her socks, to distract myself. She doesn't know what a state this park is. She only knows to see the good stuff. I wish I was like her.

Like my little duck.

The swing squeaks, creaks and clunks. I listen to it. The rhythm. The screech of the swing's chains. Chloë's feet flap. And the swing goes:

Squeak, creak,
Up and down.

I don't feel as bad, when I think about the music, the song I can write in my mind, to the swing beat and Chloë's feet. I imagine mixing the squeak, creak, with the beat of Chloë's Five Little Ducks song.

My friends are over there, chatting about last night and next week and all the things they can do with their lives right now and later. Meanwhile, all I can do, is think about Chloë and a song:

> *"My little duck is swinging today,*
> *When I push her high, she can see far away,*
> *All around me people go quack, quack,*
> *Me and little duck will soon have to swim back."*

It's not the greatest. I'm just getting started. And it's too self-conscious-making to start mouthing the lyrics and really thinking about the beat, while the others are opposite me.

I notice Derren dart forward - one of Chloë's socks has fallen off. Derren puts the sock back on Chloë's foot and tickles her toes. Chloë giggles, loving it. I imagine the sound of her giggle, sampled, sitting between sections of my song.

What verse can I write next?

I listen to the squeak, creak of the swing. Drop down into it.

Derren has stayed on this side with us. He can hear the beat too – the squeak, creak, up and down. He makes a more tuneful version with it, that comes from the corner of his mouth and the middle of his throat, all at the same time:

"Eeeeeerk, urrrrrrrrk."

Derren stands in front of Chloë's swing. We gently push her back and forth between us. He says, "Eeeeeerk, urrrrrrrrk." I hear the paddle of the little ducks, flapping the water below them, with their flippy feet. What are the next words in me that want to come out?

"You got lyrics, Missie Misdemeanour?" Derren says, as if he knows what's in my mind right now. He beatboxes a bass line that he blends in with Eeeeeerk, urrrrrrrrk. A one-man mixing desk. He takes a couple of bars to settle into it. I glance at Shannon and Tommy – they are slowly moving back towards each other and aren't paying the slightest attention to what we are doing.

Derren's track has reached the perfect blend of swinging, creaking and bass-making. He gently pushes Chloë's swing towards me and nods. Quietly, I go for it, as Chloë swings back and forth between us:

> *"We're little ducks, that's what all the adults say,*
> *They don't know how we daily grow up our own way,*
> *They think they're only ones allowed to quack, quack, quack,*
> *But they can't do what we do, swinging, beatboxing a track."*

Tommy and Shannon have come closer. Shannon can't help herself – she starts to move to the music we're making. Chloë flaps her arms and starts dancing too, wobbling her body in the swing. Shannon makes goo noises for Chloë. Derren adds a snare to the track. Then:

> *Eeeeeerk, urrrrrrrk.*
> *Squeak, creak.*
> *Bass, snare.*
> *Our beat.*

"Hear her now," Derren says, pretending like he's an old school MC. Tommy and Shannon close the space around us. I continue, a bit louder, pushing my voice out, as I push Chloë's swing:

> *"Growing up as a duck, we've got to act a certain way,*
> *Let the adults think that we listen to what they say,*
> *But adults aren't always right and they don't always have our back,*
> *In fact, some adults, they don't even give a quack."*
>
> *Eeeeeerk, urrrrrrrk.*
> *Squeak, creak.*

What can I write next? Shall I just let the lyrics come tumbling out, now I know the structure? I feel alive. I feel clicked into myself. So clicked in, I have failed to notice that the space around us has broken. That Derren's stopped gently pushing Chloë back. Tommy has hunched over. Shannon's got a blush on her cheeks, that's not make-up – a blush that she gets when she is worried.

And I see her. Mum. Carrying lager cans, crisps and biscuits, in a thin-to-breaking plastic bag from the shop.

She looks like she's been up all night. Her face is grey-yellow-beige. Her skin is stretched across her cheeks. She's even lost weight since last week. Whatever magic Nan made on her hair, Saturday in the salon, is all gone now. It's scraped back in the usual tight bun. She's still got last night's heels and skirt on, with his big, badman wolf coat over the top.

I stop the swing. I try to look small. I hope Mum won't notice we are here. But the change in movement alerts Mum to us. She wobbles over, trying hard to walk straight. I pull Chloë's swing towards me. The others are all watching Mum approach.

"Hello, babba," Mum waves at Chloë. I hear cigarettes and last night's shouting in Mum's voice. Chloë looks at Mum, like, who are you?

Please leave, Mum.

"Alright, you lot?" Mum's eyes are unfocused, though she is trying to make out like she can look at everyone. Mum cracks open a can and offers it around. "Want a sip?" No one responds. "Go on, I won't tell anyone," Mum adds, trying to wink, but having to really concentrate to do it.

"We're alright, Belle," Shannon says. Mum wobbles closer to Shannon and speaks with blurred and messy-sounding words:

"Look at little Shanny Shan. Haven't you grown up?"

Mum notices Tommy. "He your boyfriend?" Shannon's cheeks burn pinker. She doesn't answer. Mum leans closer to Tommy – I think of how she must stink. I wish I could tell her to go, to get away from us, to get away from my baby and my friends.

Mum puts a hand on Tommy's arm and nods back in Shannon's direction, slurring, "She's a bit of princess, you know."

Tommy wriggles, steps backwards, trying to get away.

Mum laughs.

"I'm only joking, aren't I, darling?" Mum puts an arm round Shannon. I'm so sorry, Shannon. Talking to Derren now, Mum grips Shannon tight. "I've known her since she was a baby."

A thought occurs to Mum, she tries to reach for Derren as well. "And you..." Derren dodges backwards and scoops a hand to the ground, as if he is picking something up, but really, he is getting away from Mum. Derren pretends to put something in his pocket.

I can't watch this anymore. While Mum takes another sip from her can, I pick Chloë up from the swing, turn my back on everyone and start tucking Chloë back into her buggy. We need to swim over the hill and far away and do it right now.

More words mumble and blend together from Mum's mouth, "What you all doing then?" Mum's phone bleeps and she pulls it out.

"Practising for Hold the Mic," says Derren.

I stop, partway through clicking the buggy straps round Chloë. Freeze.

No, Derren. Don't mention Hold the Mic.

But Mum is looking at her phone. It will be him. Texting his orders:

"Hurry up." Or:

"Get back now." Or:

"Get me some more cans while you're there."

Perhaps Mum didn't hear Derren... I fold Chloë's buggy canopy down, hoping, giving myself something to do, whilst I wait this part out. Mum texts back, eyes crossing, because she can't focus soberly on the screen. At last, she's leaving. And it looks like she didn't hear Derren.

But then Mum stops. She asks a question, wobbling on her heels. Her back's still to my friends, so they can't read her face:

"Hold the Mic?" This is a trick of Mum's of old. Even when she's in a state, she can hear something a minute after you said it, or reach for information from you, without you knowing what she's doing.

"Gail Force is lovely," Shannon says. Mum straightens up, keeping her back turned to us. I imagine what an ugly look she's got on her face right now - like when she saw the Hold the Mic flyers in the salon.

I know that there is nothing I can do. Mum is on to us now.

Mum's phone bleeps again. She looks at it, but she's only pretending to be interested in the screen. The question in Mum's voice sounds deliberately casual, like I tried to sound, when asking Nan about Mum and Gail Force last night:

"You all been going to this Hold the Mic, then?"

"No," I reply, quickly, hearing my voice crack with the lie - I had to jump in, before anyone else could answer.

"Oh, yeah?" says Mum. Then she points at us all, making out like she's all banter:

"You little piggies better not be lying to me..."

Please, no one tell her. No one tell the truth. Mum uses truth as a weapon.

We are all still. Chloë squawks in her buggy, which means she's hungry. Mum acts like Chloë is calling to her.

"Ah, bye, bye, darling," Mum waves her hand at Chloë. What a performance for the others. Do they know what a faker Mum is?

And then Mum turns and goes. She walks with her arms folded across her. The plastic bag of shopping is bouncing up and down against her body. I imagine his cans getting frothed up inside. I know he will punish her, if a can sprays out on his jeans, or his floor, when he opens it. And for a moment, I am glad – that she might get punished.

And then I hate myself for wishing that

on her.

And then Mum is gone.

I am still here, in the park, with my friends. We were having so much fun and now I feel like all the secrets of my life are out here for everyone to see, scattered with the rubbish on the ground. I want to cover my self back up. Get away.

"She stinks," I say – about Chloë. I double-check her straps and call over my shoulder, "See you all tomorrow."

I wheel the long way out of the park, to avoid bumping into Mum again. I switch off my phone and power walk to Nan's, desperate to be back in my hiding place.

The buggy wheels clatter loudly. We rattle across loose paving stones. I push Chloë to the place we call home, hearing another verse of my song in my head, as we go:

"I pushed my little duck, clattering, rattling away,
I couldn't stay around my friends, did not know what to say,
I feel like I cannot be heard, that silent is my quack,

I cannot swim forward, without I'm pulled right back."

CHAPTER 8

I spend the rest of Sunday feeling washed back away from any chance of a normal teenager life.

Monday, I'm loaded with so much study and work, it makes the stuff I was proud to get done last week look like a joke. I think I might just give up, stop trying.

Tuesday morning, Nan's got an email about coming in to school, to discuss their long-term concerns about me. Nan puts down her phone, after she reads the email. "It's not my business," Nan says - and that's the end of that.

Tuesday afternoon, walking Chloë home from nursery, I don't write lyrics to a buggy wheel squeak, or sing her a Twinkle, Twinkle.

No Incy Wincy for us.

Tuesday night, we've eaten tea. I'm

sitting on the bed. Chloë is bathed, pyjamas on, wriggling and ready for our songs. She's full of beans. I'm empty of everything.

What's the point in me trying, scrabbling?

I hit shuffle on the playlist and just sit there. I watch Chloë. Chloë watches me, waiting. No songs are coming, Chloë.

My phone's still in my hand, when the group chat starts beeping.

I quickly switch my phone to silent, because I don't want Chloë to get distracted from falling asleep. I watch the chat roll out.

SHANNON:	Ready?
DERREN:	Ready
SHANNON:	Meet at Missie's?

No, no, no. I try to fire up my slow, tired mind. I need to type, divert them away from collecting me. And quickly.

DERREN:	Yep

No!

SHANNON: I'm almost there.

I can't think fast enough.

SHANNON: Wait outside, I'll grab her for us.

Can I get Nan to tell them I'm not well?

Knock, knock, knock – this has always been Shannon's knock on the front door, since she was seven years old.

I will – I'll have to get Nan to tell them I'm not well. I can't think of anything else this quickly.

Nan won't do it though. She'll say something like, "Don't get me involved."

I hear Nan open her front door. I hear Nan and Shannon talk. I hold Chloë close, as Shannon knocks on my bedroom door and peeps her head round.

"I think Chloë's feeling sick," I say. "I'll have to stay here with her." But Chloë's wriggling away from me. She grins at Shannon. Nan comes in too, behind Shannon. Chloë leans out to Nan for a cuddle. Nan takes her. Chloë looks clean, shining, healthy and happy. Not at all ill.

"Get going," Nan says. "You've made enough of a fuss out of it. You're not ducking out now." Shannon smiles at me - she only hears the good bits of Nan's voice, not how put out Nan actually feels about having to look after Chloë. How Nan will moan about it all week.

Shannon links me.

Nan looks at me, passing me a meaning from her eyes. Nan's look means, go out and get on with it. Stop making a scene. Make us look normal.

So now I have to go, or Nan will sulk with me all night anyway.

I let Shannon steer me out the bedroom, down the hall, past the old photos. I don't like leaving Chloë. I don't like not wrestling the buggy out of the front door, before I go anywhere – it feels weird to be without it.

The others all chat as we walk, like they're still messaging in the group. I pretend to listen, but, really, I'm trying to find the good in the bad of tonight. I think it through:

At least I get a break from Nan.
At least I don't get sulked at.
At least I get to be around music.
And see Gail.

I'm not performing, though. No way. Nursery rhyme beats and songs about being a teen parent. It's too real.

In The Lowdown, I stand at the back with my hood up.

Gail Force and her DJ have started the beats. Nerves and excitement are tingling around the room. People are ready, have hyped themselves to participate tonight. To perform for Gail.

Derren is beatboxing in a corner, while Tommy watches him, nodding his head.

I must admit, it does affect me, this mood. I feel excited too. I feel jealous that they'll perform and I won't.

I must admit, I get my phone out and select the nursery rhymes playlist and the track I want.

I'm still not getting up there, though.

Once the session starts, other people get up and have a go on the mic – and they're mostly okay. They copy famous MCs, rip off well-known flows.

And then my lot get up in this order - Tommy, Shannon, Derren. Like they planned it, which I soon realise, watching them, they did.

They planned it and performed it for each other, when I wasn't there. Maybe on Sunday, when I rushed away from them - when I left them to their normal teenager lives, in the park.

I can't believe Tommy. He's as shy as ever, but he takes the mic in his hand – he doesn't leave it on the stand like everyone else. Straight into the mic - a stripped-back, pretty angry set of lyrics about who he is, in perfect time to the beat:

> *"Tommy,*
> *Don't try to copy me,*
> *People wanna come to me,*
> *Show you how loud a shy boy can be."*

Not bad, but that last line would improve with a word taken out, "Know how loud shy boys can be." For the flow. And then he's gone, straight off the stage, blushing. I try to catch a look with him, to say, "Well done." But he stands by the wall. Hair hanging over his face. Phone out:

TOMMY: *typing…*

And I'm going to bottle out tonight,

while Typing Tommy gets up and quietly wrecks the mic?

Shannon has the mic now. She holds her dancer's body straight. I know she is tiny, but she looks ten feet tall. She fills the space around her and glows in the light. Shannon clips the mic back to the stand. She says, "Shanny," into the mic, then she waits for the top of the next bar and starts moving.

She flips, she flicks, she does the splits. She manages something that no one else here could do.

Her moves suit the beat and warm the crowd up. And then she's gone. Everyone whoops. As Shannon glides from the stage, she gets a high five from Gail Force.

Yes, they've helped each other, talked stuff through. I sense Derren's guidance in Tommy's bars. I imagine them whooping and Tommy blushing, while Shannon danced for them in the park, after I ran away, got washed away, on Sunday.

Why can't I have a life like that? Why can't I be a normal teenager? Maybe then, I wouldn't be sitting here, with my stupid nursery rhyme track on the phone in my hand, trying to find the guts to get up there and make a fool of myself. Maybe I'd be writing lyrics about school and exams and normal stuff that normal people can relate to.

And then, Derren steps up. He's prepped, he's ready. He doesn't look nervous one bit. He does a dip and roll move to the mic, unclips it and holds it at the top. He makes some extra beats, deep into the microphone, with his voice. They pop and fizz with the track that the DJ is playing. People are getting to their feet. After a while, Derren clips the mic back in and stands at it, leaning in. His hands are behind his back, like he's an old guy waiting for a bus.

"Oweeeeeeeee, D-Damager,"

Derren's developing a nice, little sound effect to announce himself. It makes people want to listen to him.

> *"When I when I when I when I went to primary school,*
> *I was a wink murderer,*
> *(Oweeeeeeeee, D-Damager),*

Now you need to see,
That I'm a microphone slayer."

This is a total Derren flow – so much old school in there.

Derren executes a classic pop-and-lock move. Effortless, shrugged off.

I remember Derren when he was seven and still used to come to dancing lessons - before all the boys got too old and too cool and stopped coming. He's always had moves. Derren dips and rolls away from the mic, moving backwards, reversing everything. Everyone is on their feet and so am I. The room's pumped. The next few average people ride on the wave of Derren's brilliance.

I stand there, hood up.

Shall I, though?

If I don't, all these words in me have nowhere to go. I'll go back to Nan's, feeling worse than I already did, when I set off.

I want to feel better. I want to pretend I can be normal, if only for a few minutes, on a cold Tuesday in The Lowdown.

I approach the stage, phone in hand, hood staying up, so I can't see people around me. I give my phone to the DJ, show him the track. He looks surprised, but then plugs in the phone and starts mixing the track in. I can hear the plinky, plinky nursery rhyme start to blend with the DJ's beat.

The DJ nods at me – as in, all yours.

Time to hold the mic.

My heart goes thump, thump, thump. My mouth is so dry, but my skin is so damp – both caused by pure fear. This microphone is weighty in my hand. I could run? But the shame of that, in front of everyone.

I could go for it? But, if I choke, the shame of that too, in front of everyone.

I think about Chloë. I picture her rolling on Nan's spare room carpet, while I perform. I imagine it's me and her together, alone. I imagine she's loving me performing for her. I breathe in and pretend Chloë is right in front of me:

> *"This little miss,*
> *Is no muffet,*
> *Is no muppet,*
> *Not down here,*
> *On some fluffy tuffet,*

Need to stay sharp,
Need to stay real,
You know me,
Yes, I'm the baby girl."

I step back. Microphone rocking on the stand. Boom, boom, boom, goes my heart and the beat. People are looking. Did I just do that?

Wait, people are grinning and someone whoops and then there are some hollers.

Gail Force takes the mic from me, saying into it, "It's Missie, everyone!" Gail accidentally knocks my hood down, as she puts an arm round me. I feel so hot with sweat and fear, it's kind of a relief to have my head exposed. I don't put my hood back up.

Gail must be able to feel me shaking, to smell me perspiring. Derren, Shannon and Tommy are waiting by the wall. Shannon hugs me. Derren fist-bumps me. Tommy nods, actually looking me in the eye.

I slide down the wall and sit on the floor. I try to make it look intentional, but I don't have a choice - my legs can't hold me up any longer.

We break for juice, crisps, talking about beats. People pass me and say, "Nice," or nod at me. Everyone is friendly. It feels like we are all the same. But only for a minute.

I start to feel weird, as I remember I'm not like everyone else. I feel sad - like tears might come. I want the night to be over. I feel I'm a fool for saying the things about myself that I said on the stage.

I'm quiet, all through the second half of the evening. Gail chats to the group. She plays some tracks and talks about them. I sink deep in my mind. My hood goes back up. I want to be alone. When it's home time, I take ages putting on my jacket, fiddling with the frayed laces on my Stan Smiths, like I can't do them up. Ignoring my friends, while they wait for me by the door.

I just can't be around anyone, after showing my full self like that.

Eventually, they get the message. Shannon calls over, "See you tomorrow!" But I don't answer. I'm closed now for the day.

Goodbye normal teenagers.

The lights come on. Gail Force and the DJ are packing down. When they're done and she hugs him goodbye, Gail calls to me, "You going home, Missie?"

I feel so stupid, standing here. What was I thinking, coming here and holding the mic, like I'm a Gail Force type?

Gail puts the lights out and moves to the door to lock up and leave. I follow her.

"That was great tonight, Missie," Gail says. We walk down the path and the bike lads move, giving us plenty of space, without being asked.

"A nursery rhyme?" I sputter my words out. I hate the sound of my voice right now.

"Yes," Gail says. "You were real." It feels like our chat is coming to an end. But I want to stay near Gail and to hear more about music from her. To hear kind words. To see if I dare ask Gail, how she knows me.

"I've got no other beats," I say, quietly. I follow Gail across the square, wanting to stay near her, to hear more from her.

"It's the sign of a true artist – making something from nothing." Gail says. We are at the shop now. Gail is looking at me, like I'm going to follow her in.

But I've stopped. "True artist?" I say.

"Yes, you are," Gail says.

That is not something I have ever

thought of myself as. I smile. I decide to follow Gail into the shop and talk to her more about music. I decide I will pluck up the courage to ask her my question:

"How do you know me?" I think it to myself, as if to a beat.

Then, bleep, the shop door sounds, as we go in.

Oh. My question evaporates.

My smile fades.

Mum and him are at the counter.

He's shaking hands with the shop owner, but it's more of a threat, than a sign of friendship. She's fidgeting behind him. Gail notices them. I don't know what Gail knows and what Mum knows and what he knows and what I am supposed to know. Because I still don't know anything.

I think about running. He will see me. Can I hide? Too late. They're saying their goodbyes and leaving. Him first, hands in his big, badman wolf coat pockets. Mum behind him, baa, baa. Carrying the beers, the food – yes sir, yes sir, three bags full.

They see us. He stops and Mum stops behind him. He flicks his internal badman switch, powers up to 100%.

And he laughs. Big and deep. It goes on and on. I know he could do anything next. There is no way to predict him.

"Look at you two," he says. His eyes are on me, giving me a look. I know what it means. It means:

KEEP YOUR MOUTH SHUT.

I can see the shopkeeper is watching, pretending not to be watching, glad not to be the focus of his stare. The big, badman wolf takes his hands from his pockets and leaves. Swinging his arms. Swagger. He's gone from the shop. Mum turns quickly back and whispers to Gail:

"You shouldn't've come back."

Gail's eyes get bigger, but she doesn't speak. What would she say, if she did speak back to Mum?

Mum hurries away, heavy bags swinging from her thin arms - baa, baa - after her three-bags-full master.

Why does Mum think she can say something like that to Gail Force? I feel embarrassed, yet again, to be her daughter.

Gail and I leave the shop - without

buying anything, without speaking to, or looking at, each other. At the path to Nan's, Gail says, "Goodnight." Then she is gone.

I'm so full of questions that I hardly sleep. The beat to these questions, is my own heart thumping. My worried blood rushes, with the certainty that there is more to this situation.

The words race through my brain:

> *"How do you know me?*
> *Why do they hate you?*
> *Why am I lonely?*
> *Why did Mum say that to you?"*

On and on 'til morning.

CHAPTER 9

All the next day at school, my stomach is a hard, painful knot. Those questions stopped me sleeping and I know something is coming, after Mum and him saw Gail and me, at the shop last night.

So, when Mum's outside Nan's, after school, I feel weirdly glad - we're getting on with it and I don't have to wait and worry.

"Why are you late?" Mum barks at me. She's not a sheep now. She's his attack dog.

Woof, woof - that's what I hear, when Mum speaks. I know soon, I won't be able to fight back for any small piece of myself, so I take the chance now, to speak:

"We're not late. We get home this time every day."

Mum shows her teeth a bit: "This isn't your home."

I wish that I could shoo Mum away. One of Chloë's nursery rhymes pops into my head:

"How much is that doggy in the window."

Ridiculous to think of baby songs here and now. I smile.

"What are you laughing at?" Mum barks louder.

You – I want to say – but don't. Because Mum's bite is worse than her bark. And Chloë is watching us with big, worried eyes. I drop my smile, to avoid annoying Mum even more.

Mum's phone bleeps – she has it on the loudest setting, so she can always hear, when he contacts her. Mum checks her screen, biting her nails, eyes flicking about. I watch her. She's probably already been gone longer than she told him she would be.

What's it like being an attack dog, then a lapdog, then a bad dog? What's it like, all the time flicking between the different doggy settings? Mum is his pet, not his partner.

Mum looks up from her screen, like she

can hear me thinking about her. "Want a picture?" Yap, yap. She points at Nan's front door. "Get it open," Mum says, but all I hear is:

"Yap, yap, yap."

I need to stall for time, until Nan gets home from her Wednesday at Marcia's salon. Perhaps Nan can talk Mum out of whatever she's planning?

"I haven't got keys," I say. Mum snaps at me. Baring her yellow teeth, stepping forward and breathing her dental decay at me.

"Liar."

"I'm not." Mum grabs my school bag from me, hurting my shoulder as she yanks it. I let her take it.

Chloë is looking at me, her eyes are asking me what's happening. I reach down and stroke her face. I try to make my eyes warm, as I smile at her. She gives me a little smile back. A smile like a question. I nod back to her and keep stroking her face.

Mum is ragging through my school bag, looking for my keys to Nan's. I have a couple of minutes of thinking time – Mum's not going to find anything in there, because the keys are in my pocket. What has Mum been sent to say? To do? Is she going to ban me from Hold the Mic? What will I say when she does?

Mum gets sick of looking through my bag and tips the contents on the ground. She shakes the bag empty, then throws it over her shoulder. It lands on next-door's path. I think about how much of Mum's ruckus Nan's neighbours have witnessed, over the years.

"I know you've got a key," Mum says, then leaps forward and grabs me. I curl inwards, waiting for the slaps. But then, Mum suddenly lets me go.

Mum has seen Nan, coming down the passageway, carrying a load of shopping bags. Hair done. Looking happy. Looking sober. I think how this might have turned out to be a nice afternoon, with a happy Nan and Chloë. Nan looks like she was thinking the same, but then she spots Mum. Nan's face flickers with surprise, then she forces a smile back on, but a bigger one than before – a fake one.

"Hello Belle darling," Nan says, in her high-pitched, too-sweet, talking-to-Mum voice. Chloë looks at Nan, at Mum, at me – she knows this is not right at all.

Nan goes for the normal approach,

which has never worked in all the years I've been watching her try it. "You come for tea?" Nan says, holding up her shopping bags. "I've got plenty in."

Yes, Nan. Mum's come for tea and we're all going to sit and have a normal family meal and talk about our normal lives.

Mum shrugs. Urgh. That shrug. I feel sick whenever I see her do it. That's the shrug I got from her. I hate that parts of me are like parts of her. I wish I was nothing at all like her.

Nan is standing there, with her shopping, wondering what to say next. Then Mum blurts out her reason for being here. Everything changes for me and Chloë, as Mum says the next four words:

"They're coming with me."

Nan looks at us quickly, then looks away. Back to Mum. Nan puts her bags down and reaches out to touch Mum's arm, speaking high and false:

"What do you mean, darling?"

Mum points at us, as she speaks, "They're coming to the flat. Today. Now."

Nan steps closer to Mum and speaks quietly to her, as if we can't hear. "Belle, love,"

Nan says. "They're better off here."

Please, Mum. Please. Listen to Nan.

But Mum shrugs again. She looks at the ground, saying, "It's not up to me."

Nan sighs and hugs Mum - and I know me and Chloë are lost.

This is how it always goes. Nan lets Mum do whatever she wants. Nan never tells Mum no. Nan's going to let Mum take us. She's going to watch us go.

Nan unlocks the front door and Mum follows. I stay out on the pavement with Chloë.

Nan points to the shopping bags on the ground and says to me, "Bring those in, will you?" Then Nan puts her arm round Mum, guiding her in, through the hall. "Let's talk about it inside," Nan says to Mum, softly. Softer than she ever speaks to me, or even to Chloë.

I gather up my schoolbooks, pens and paper from the ground. I hook Nan's shopping bags on the buggy. I think through my options.

I could wheel away now? I could get Chloë out of here?

But how far would I get? I don't have a scrap of cash on me.

I could go to Shannon's? But she's at

dancing and her Mum's at work – no one's in and Mum will know to look there anyway.

In the hall, Nan and Mum have stopped. Nan takes Mum by the shoulders and looks her in the eyes. "Tell me what it is love," Nan says.

"Kyren says it's time she came home," Mum says, gesturing at Chloë and me, out on Nan's path. Home? What a joke. Don't get distracted by it, though. Think. Is there another way out?

I could call the police?

And say what? They'll call social services and then they'll start asking all those questions again. About Chloë and me. They'll take her from me.

We can't be parted.

Mum comes back to Nan's front door. "Get in here," she snarls through her teeth. And, as all the other choices aren't really choices, I go in.

Nan gives me a look that means my feelings don't matter. "Get your stuff," Nan says, then she follows Mum into the kitchen. I go into Nan's spare room. I wish I could hide in here, get in the wardrobe with Chloë, until Mum's gone.

Chloë needs a nappy change, so I bend and do it. Chloë is watching me the whole time, asking me questions with her eyes, holding her feet with her bum in the air – what a little duck she is.

Is this how Nan sees Mum? Her little duck. Did Nan sing to Mum when she was a baby? Does Nan love Mum the way I love Chloë? Is that why Nan's letting Mum take us? Mum matters more to Nan than anyone else does?

Mum barges into the spare room and barks at us, "Get moving!" Mum texts, stressed. Her phone, loud, bleeps straight back. I see Mum's eyes widen, as she reads his latest message. Her time's running out.

Which means, our time's running out too – mine and Chloë's.

Nan comes in and stuffs clothes and nappies into carrier bags. "Okay," she says to Mum. "They're ready."

"Let's go, then," Mum says, walking to the kitchen, picking up the bags full of shopping that Nan just bought. I see Chloë's milk and food in there, so at least I know my baby can eat. Mum goes outside. Nan hurries behind Mum, the same way Mum always hurries behind him.

"Come on, Missie," Nan snaps at me, looking back into her house from the path. I get the baby in the buggy and, as I push Chloë towards Nan and Mum, it's like pushing against heaviness. I can't do it.

Mum's phone bleeps three times, quickly. She glances at it, then at me and Chloë. Mum marches back for the buggy. She dumps the shopping bags and grabs Chloë's handles from me. Off she marches, wheeling Chloë away too violently, over the kerbs and bumps.

I wish I could yell at her, "Get the hell away from my baby!"

"Belle, wait!" Nan shouts and then scuttles, grabbing the shopping. I scrabble. Mum and Chloë and the buggy rattle. Our bags full of stuff dangle from Nan's arms. I take the bags from Nan - she looks worn out - I feel bad for her and hate her, all at the same time.

As we hurry behind Mum, I feel Nan put a hand in my pocket. I look down. Money is sticking out from my coat. Nan puts her finger to lips and then pushes the notes right in, so they are out of Mum's sight.

We walk across the square. People passing. We look like four female generations going about their business. Like we want to be together. Like we are a family.

We get to the bottom of the stairs by his block. Nan stops and puts the bags down. Mum goes up, leaving Chloë without looking back.

"Nan," I say. My voice is so quiet. I wish Nan would put an arm round me and talk to me, help me, the way she helps Mum.

"I'll wait here with the baby, while you take the stuff up," Nan says, meaning, don't ask for my help. I imagine Nan, home in half an hour. Telly on, fizzy wine drinking. Blocking the thought of us out. Her house to herself again, how she likes it.

"Give me the spare keys as well," Nan says, holding out a hand. "There'll be murder, if you sneak back to my house."

Nan - how can you? I hand the keys back, with a sick feeling rising in me. Me and Chloë are trapped.

I carry the bags up the stairs, along the walkway – the plastic handles dig into my hands. I pass other flats – telly on, music, chatting. Please, could I go through any of these front doors instead?

The light is on outside his flat, so people know he's home. His TV blares out onto the walkway. Booms and crashes from some action film. He doesn't care what the neighbours think.

I leave the bags on the border to his world - smelling sweat and dirt, weed and cigarettes, as I bend to place them. That familiar, big, badman wolf odour.

I go back down for the buggy. As I reach the bottom step, Nan turns on her heel and hurries away, across the square. Leaving us to it.

I could go too? Run away with Chloë? Now is our best chance of escaping.

"Hurry up!" Mum is leaning over the walkway - her eyes popping, her neck straining, her voice like nails, scratching hard, in my head.

I take Chloë out of the buggy, balance her on my hip and collapse the buggy down. I hook the buggy over my arm and carry myself, buggy and baby. We go up the stairs, to the flat.

Mum goes back in, eyes nervous and wide, as I reach the top step.

Chloë is sliding down me. I hitch her up.

She whimpers.

"Ssssh, ssssh," I say. Then, to calm her, to make her as quiet as possible. I whisper to her, as we get closer to the flat, like this is all a game:

"One step, Two step..."

And then, we are there.

CHAPTER 10

It's gone silent. But, even if the light wasn't on over his front door, I would know he's there. In the flat.

He can send badness out far from him, when he wants you to know that he's watching, or waiting.

The big, badman wolf.

I feel small again, stepping into his flat. I think of when I was little – Mum pulling my arm, more than holding my hand, as she took me to live with him. I hitch Chloë up, tighten my arms around her, get her as snug as I can, on my hip.

"I love you," I whisper to her. Chloë's the child now. I'm the grown-up, the one who looks out for her. I have to be brave for us both.

I hear Mum talking to him in the lounge. She's squeaking and he's grumbling, in a low, deep voice. His power. Her fear. It's like music, that they've danced to so many times - and I've been outside in the hall listening to it so many times too.

Can Chloë hear their music? Does it scare her, like it scares me? I hum How Much is that Doggy in the Window. Close to Chloë's ear. To soothe her. I wish I could pull up her playlist on my phone and perform a track for her, to help her feel safe.

"What's she doing out there?" He shouts. Mum's head appears from the lounge door. She waves us in, her face scrunched, her eyes darting about. I leave the buggy, folded up on the floor in the hall and walk in behind Mum, with Chloë.

Mum scurries back – yap, yap – to perch on the arm of his chair. His throne. But he waves her away, so she sits on the floor. She's at his feet. Near his thick legs, which are set apart, taking up as much space as he can.

He should get her a basket.

The How Much is that Doggy track plays in my head. Then a lyric pops into my mind alongside it:

"What's up with this doggy in the flat, though?"

I'm looking at them, but in my mind I'm searching for the next line I can write to a Doggy in the Window beat. It helps my heart to stop whomp, whomp, whomping.

He growls, low, deep and powerful, "Welcome home." And then he laughs.

He laughs.

He laughs more. I can hear cigarettes and phlegm in him. I can hear his powerful ribcage. The way he shouts, the looks he gives. The big, badman wolf's big, badman laugh.

Mum's getting twitchy. She stands. I can tell she wants to move him on from all this laugh, laugh, laughing. She picks up Nan's shopping bags.

"Got us tea, babe," Mum says, waving the bags like they're a trophy. Mum empties the shopping onto their messy table. There's tea, sugar, biscuits, tins, packets, cheese, milk. Mum doesn't empty the bag with Chloë's milk, food and nappies in - she puts that bag quietly under the table. He doesn't notice.

He picks up the remote control. "Get cooking, then," he says. He waves the controller, as if batting Mum away. "Move," he says, as he switches on the TV.

Mum goes to the kitchen area. "Get in the corner," he says, meaning Chloë and me. I sit at the table with Chloë, far enough back, so she can't reach any of the ashtrays, empty cans, papers, tobacco, takeaway cartons and whatever else is hidden in all this mess.

Mum microwaves beans, while he stares at the telly. She tips the beans on bread, crumbles crisps and cheese on the top and serves it to him, with a small plate of digestives, a mug of tea and two ciders. Urgh.

I'm still writing that song in my head, hoping Chloë can tell I am sending her a musical signal:

> *"What's up with this doggy in the flat, though?*
> *Mum's cooking and wagging her tail."*

At this point, the song on Chloë's playlist would go:

"Woof, woof."

He's now slopping and scoffing his food. Mum's sitting watching, like she's hoping for a scrap. I continue making the track in my mind:

> *"Her master's not one for sharing food, though,*
> *So doggy stays hungry and pale,*
> *Woof, woof."*

When did Mum last eat a proper meal? She used to have curves. She was slim, but she had shape. Lines. She had in and out sections at her hips and thighs and waist. She would look good and people would look at her looking good. She looked like a real person.

But he took all that. He took the actual food from her mouth. Now she just waits for his leftovers.

"Woof, woof," I think.

Chloë and I stay in the corner, at the table, all evening - waiting for them to go to bed. Eventually, Chloë falls asleep on me. Every time my arm aches with her weight, I slowly move her – just a little bit, trying not to attract his attention. Poor, hungry baby's had no dinner. And nor have I.

I didn't have lunch either. My stomach was sloshing about too much, but I'm starting to really feel the hunger now.

Standing with Gail Force, seeing Mum and him in the shop last night, feels days ago.

He drinks more cans, gobs off about whatever's on telly:

"She's a daft cow."

"Look at this prick."

"I could do better than that."

So many opinions.

Mum curls up at his feet, leaning on his thigh. He rests his hand on her bony head, as he watches TV. Meanwhile, I write the next part of my song, in my mind:

> *"Why is it that doggy lives this life, though?*
> *It feels like it's kind of a trap,*
> *Woof, woof,*
> *This doggy's always yapping, flapping,*
> *scared, though,*
> *If she's a bad dog, she's getting a slap,*
> *Woof, woof."*

It's fully dark outside now. There are no curtains, or blinds, on his flat windows. I can see the reflection of Mum and him, as they stare at the telly. The lights of the programmes flicker across their faces.

Three cans in, he stands. He pulls his trackies up, puts his trainers on - the latest kicks, though they look ugly on him. He belches, then goes to the bathroom.

He leaves the door open. A long, splashing stream, with a fart at the end of it. Mum is still sitting on the floor, head on the chair that he's vacated. Her eyes track him moving around, out in the hall.

He comes to the lounge door – filling all the space in the frame with his big, badman wolf coat. He points at me, growling, low. "Don't move," he says.

Mum stands up and whimpers a question:

"Am I coming, babe?"

"Nah," he replies. I hear him pick up keys and coins, from the shelf in the hall. Then the flat front door opens. Mum pads out quickly, calling to him, as he leaves:

"I'll keep the bed warm, babe!"

In the room, alone for a minute, I write another verse, saying this one out loud:

> *"Oh, why is that doggy calling out though?*
> *They don't even sound like real words,*
> *Woof, woof,*
> *The flats hear her howling, barking, don't go,*
> *We all know she'll never be heard,*
> *Woof, woof."*

Mum must still be out on the walkway – I can feel the cold of the night air coming in, reaching us in our corner. Chloë stirs. I hold her closer, try to pass some warmth from me to her. I picture Mum, leaning out and watching the big, badman wolf walking across the square. Mum comes back in, clicking the front door shut. From the hallway, she snarls at me:

"Happy now?"

I can't see Mum's face from here, but I know it will be twisted, angry, hating us. Mum clatters about in the bathroom, annoyed. Then she goes to their bedroom and closes the door, tight.

I know that sound so well. So many nights, when I was little, I lay alone, on an airbed, in that hall. I'd hear their bedroom door shut me out. No one ever wishing me goodnight.

Chloë is deeply asleep. Her mouth looks juicy and soft. Her face is smooth. I feel bad that she's missed out on a bedtime nursery rhyme track. I hope I can perform a goodnight song for her tomorrow.

But, if we're still here, how is that going to happen? I'm not lonely, because Chloë is here, but I feel alone. I feel like a question is starting to creep up on me, now that I'm not concentrating on being as quiet and still as possible:

What are me and Chloë going to do now?

Okay, I can't think about that. I pick Chloë up and move to the sofa. I put Chloë across my lap, both arms hooked around her, so she can't roll off.

I look at the kitchen area. I can see it better from here. It's filthy. The walls are stained with oil and steam and tobacco. There are cobwebs and dust. There are spiders.

But I can't distract myself enough - the question is still hanging there, stuck like one of those kitchen cobwebs:

What are me and Chloë going to do now?

I know we can't do anything, but sit and sleep and wait. We're trapped. We're stuck in his cobweb.

I can feel myself getting hot, my mouth getting dry, panicking. I'm so tired, but how will I ever sleep here, with Chloë to keep safe now as well? No, I can't think about that. About being stuck. About being caught in a web.

If a spider is what I am, then I have to be a different kind of spider. I have to work with what me and Chloë have got.

I start to hum, as quietly as I can. Incy Wincy. Over and over. Eventually, I feel sleepy enough to let my head rest on my shoulder. Just a few minutes to close my eyes, sitting up, on this sofa.

I wake to the sound of the front door clanging open in the night. My neck hurts. In three steps, he is standing over me and Chloë. He's breathing through his mouth in the dark room. People on the telly are in leather chairs, in some studio, talking to each other like everything's normal.

Meanwhile, the fabric of his joggers is almost touching my face. He stinks of the pub. Of sweat and weed. I know I have to keep absolutely still, if I don't want to suffer tonight.

Think hard of those nursery rhymes. Keep your head there. Lyrics. Words. Beats. It's hard, in this state of mind - all I can pull up, is the last image that was in my head. Cobwebs, a stuck spider. Think of a song, quick:

"Incy Wincy Spider..."

He puts his hand on top of my skull, his fingers pressing into my head. "Do not try anything with me," he says.

I stay still. I stay silent, small. Hiding in the waterspout.

He twists and pulls some of my hair, tight, my eyes stretching with the pressure.

"I'm the boss around here," he says. I feel the pulse of his breath, it's bouncing off the top of my head. "I'm the king," he says.

He doesn't move. And nor do I. I'm starting to think stillness isn't going to work. It feels like he's preparing and then will suddenly attack. Bam. That's how he goes.

Then Mum calls out to him from the hallway, "Babe?" She's in her underwear. He looks up. His grip on my hair loosens.

"You coming, babe?" Mum doesn't sound like a desperate, yappy dog now. He drops my hair and walks towards her.

She's distracting him.

"I'm the king," he growls back at me. Then he gets hold of Mum and they go into their bedroom.

I don't know if I sleep, or if I just exist in the waterspout in my mind. Eventually, light comes from outside, as dawn approaches. Everything is quiet in the room next door. I get the buggy and my schoolbag and carefully strap sleeping Chloë in. I need to get out, into this new day, quickly, but very quietly.

Slowly, I wheel to the door. I open it, without making a sound. We're on the walkway and I've almost got the door shut, when it's yanked from my hand.

He is standing there, naked. I step back. "See you later," he says and then starts with his laughing again.

Ha. Ha. Ha.

I speed down the walkway, wheels

rolling, him laughing in the morning air behind us. I carry the whole lot - buggy, baby and all - down the steps to the ground floor in one go. It kills my back, but the fear carries me forward.

I wheel and run across the square - desperate to get away, even though I know I have to come back here later. He's out on the balcony, still naked, still the king. He bellows to us:

"See you later!"

He laughs more and more, the sound echoing off the walls of the other flats.

I run down the pavements. I swerve round the corners. I leave the streets where I have played and lived and walked to school.

We reach a different area. Painted doors. Gardens with plants. A park with trees and benches. Chloë starts to wake up, as I click open a metal gate to a brightly painted play area, in this nice and happy park.

There is a little wooden climbing frame, with ropes on the roof, made to look like a cottage from a fairy tale. It has a bench inside. I take Chloë from her buggy and sit her in the fairy tale cottage with me.

She puts her hand on my cheek and I feel

a tear drop from me to her.

What are me and Chloë going to do now?

CHAPTER 11

I sit Chloë on my lap, facing outwards. I wrap her up warm, in her buggy blanket. I want to cry so much, but I don't want to worry my baby. I want her to feel safe.

I look around me. What can I focus on, to stop getting upset? There are words, from nursery rhymes and fairy tales. They're printed around the walls, inside the playhouse:

"Once upon a time..."

"They huffed and they puffed..."

"Round and round the garden..."

"Run, run, as fast as you can..."

Chloë is looking around too – looking around and then looking at me. I say to her, like I'm so happy:

"We are inside a song!"

I jig her up and down, up and down. What's that fussy tune, about riding a horse to some cross? It's near the end of Chloë's playlist and we don't often bother with it. I wish I knew it now, so I could make a tune, like a horse. Jig Chloë up and down, up and down.

What are me and Chloë going to do now?

We're going to make music together.

I take out my phone.

It's dead.

I wish my phone had battery.

Wishes. You make them in fairy tales, don't you? Those types of stories, where there's a genie, or a fairy, or some half-good, half-bad old lady, who's hobbling down the road. She can grant you wishes, make your dreams come true – at a price. Well, I would pay that price now, whatever it was, for one magic wish.

I wouldn't waste a magic wish on asking for phone battery, though.

I think of what I wished for as a kid. It was always something to do with Mum. I'd wish she would:

Hug me.

Take me to the park.

Come back, from whatever place she'd gone to, and take me to live with her.

Now, I wish she would:

Vanish - in a puff of smoke.

Chloë arches her back, tetching at me. She's been sitting still for ages. She must be so hungry. She must be so confused. She must feel how I felt growing up.

I don't want this life for Chloë. I'm changing my wish. I'm not wasting it on making Mum vanish. I wish:

I could make this fairy tale cottage into a little home for me and Chloë. A carpet, a telly, a cooker, a bath and a bed. Warm blankets and a radiator.

But, in a way, it feels like I am wishing for the same kinds of things I always wished for. Not fairy tale stuff at all. Just normal, everyday stuff.

Is Chloë going to grow up wishing she was normal? Is she going to wish I would vanish one day, in a puff of magic smoke?

Chloë is starting to cry. Like she's hungry, but also too hungry to get really annoyed about it.

I wish I could feed her. Oh, stop wishing.

Start thinking. Start doing.

I've got half a chocolate bar that Shannon gave me the other day – she only ever eats half a chocolate bar. Thank you, Shannon - it's just a little wish granted, but it's all we need right now.

I move Chloë, so she's facing me. I make an Incy, Wincy game. Each time the spider climbs her waterspout, Chloë gets a bit more chocolate. A tiny bit. She gets happy – with the singing and the sugar. Her mushy mouth turns chocolatey. I stretch out the game, and the chocolate, as long as I can.

What Chloë really needs is baby rice, or mashed-up cereal with warm milk. She needs her nappy changing. Her soft skin wiping and letting to the air, so she doesn't get a rash. Well, there's no point in wishing for that, because I can't make it come true.

What are me and Chloë going to do? We're going to think practically and I'm going to get us out of this right now, too cold, early morning damp, sitting-in-a-playpark-in-winter situation. It's all I can change, for the moment.

A man and woman walk past, cutting through the park. They are holding hands, dressed smartly and heading somewhere, like they are looking forward to it. I guess they're on their way to work? I could ask them for help?

I stand up and leave the fairy tale cottage with Chloë. My back aches, as I uncurl myself, while holding Chloë's weight. "Excuse me," I say. They stop. They turn back. The woman lets go of the man's hand and steps back towards us.

"Are you okay?" The woman asks. Her voice sounds kind. I think about replying:

"No, we're really not okay."

But then the man pulls on her coat. "Jen, come on," he says. He wants her to keep moving. Is he a three-bags-full master as well? I don't want Jen to get hurt later, for helping us now. I nod my head and push back the words that I thought about saying. I put Chloë in her buggy, my back to them, like it's no big deal. I'm just normal, like them.

But I feel a touch on my shoulder. It burns. I jump back, flinch, quickly. Get ready to run.

It's the woman. Jen. She is looking at me and Chloë the way adults look at us, when they are trying to work out what our story is.

I need to get my baby away from her.

I wish I'd never said anything.

I smile back, like I'm a normal parent. I think of a question. "Do you know what time it is?" I ask. The woman looks at her watch.

"It's 7.30," she says. "In the morning," she adds, like I don't know. Then she says, "It's early." I can see she is thinking about asking me something else. She is really near me. I feel crowded. I feel my breath speed up, as I start to get scared of what might happen next. The man calls out to her:

"Jen, we're going to be late."

She looks back at him. Then at us. Then at him.

I'm panicking now. What if she calls the police, or social services? What if she *is* the police, or social services? Why did I open my mouth to speak to these people?

What are me and Chloë going to do now?

I wish we could disappear.

Well, we can. I can make this one wish come true, if I play it right.

I'm going to act as normal as possible, while inside running faster than the gingerbread man. I stand straighter and Jen steps away, giving us more space. I look to both sides quickly - we will exit to the left, once I've got these buggy straps done.

"We were just playing before nursery," I say. Straps done. Click. Stand behind the buggy. Ready to go.

"Is this your little girl?" The woman bends down to Chloë. I want to slam the buggy into this Jen woman now, to get her away from us. I watch her notice Chloë's mushy mouth. I reach down over the back of the buggy and wipe away the chocolate with my blazer sleeve.

"She's my sister," I say, hating myself for the lie. I picture me and Chloë – Gingerbread Mum and Baby, wheeling at full speed, down a path in a fairy tale land. The woman chasing after us.

The man steps towards us now as well. Soon we will be blocked in – and they look fit and strong. It's now, or never. I make a break for the left-hand exit, calling back over my shoulder:

"We have to go to nursery now, or we'll be late." I keep moving - being quick, acting slow. Run, run, I think. Walk, walk, I go. I keep my head down.

From the sides of my eyes, I see they are still watching us, Jen and the man. I get us out of the playpark gate. Then out of the whole park. Chloë's wheels glide smoothly across this posh place pavement, even though we are now moving really quickly.

One step, two step. I speed up. Wheel, run, as fast as you can.

What are me and Chloë going to do now?

We are not going to ask any adults for help.

CHAPTER 12

"Baby Girl!" They shout at school, even though I stick to the edges of the corridor, trying to remain unseen.

I see the others in our form room. Derren is standing. He's chatting to the group he's with, while also acting to the whole room. Shannon - new bobble, glossy hair, looking beautiful - is sitting on her desk, showing something on her phone to the girls behind her. Tommy is sitting with Derren's group, but so that he can look past them and watch Shannon.

I know now, I've been kidding myself, since I came back to school - I don't belong in their world anymore. I can no longer even badly fake being a normal teenager.

So, when Shannon sees me and does her

daily grin and wave, I put my head down. I take the back seat in the corner - the seat that no one ever uses. I turn myself away from the room, pretending to look at my phone that still has no battery.

Shannon waits for me outside form, once registration is over. I dip to the side and keep walking, fast. She catches up to me and tries to link me. I keep my arm tight to my side.

"Missie? What's happened?" Shannon whispers. I speed up. But Shannon can keep pace with me - she's strong and fast, like I wish I was.

"Is Chloë okay?" Shannon asks. I don't answer.

"Has your Mum done something?" I am now walking so quickly, my feet are pounding into the floor. Shannon touches me on the arm, gently, but I pull away sharply, as if she's burned me.

Shannon stops. "Is it him?" She asks. I know I can't get into the topic of him with Shannon. He's on to me now. I can't say anything to anyone. Even my best friend.

I keep walking. Legs burning, stepping to a rapid rhythm in my head:

"Run, run, as fast as you can..."

I can't lie to Shannon. And I can't tell her the truth. I know she wants to protect me, but, if she tells anyone anything, they will take Chloë away from me.

Run, run, I go. I leave Shannon behind. As fast as I can.

I get a new timetable. I've been moved into all the struggling groups, because Nan didn't come in, to discuss my lack of progress. I'm glad. It means I don't have to avoid my friends all day. I sit at the back, in the corner, in every class - and no one cares.

It's chaos, where I am now. Loads of spiders getting washed down the waterspout of their end days of Year 11 at school. I belong with them. Everyone in these groups is abnormal, in their own unique way.

I repeat the pattern of ignoring my friends in form, for the rest of the week, until Shannon no longer tries to catch my eye, or talk to me. I feel awful, but it has to be done. If Shannon's close, she'll work something out - about how me and Chloë are living. She might even work out everything.

At the flat, it's a prison and Mum tells me the rules, whenever he's out:

"Kyren says keep your mouth shut, if anyone asks you anything."

"Kyren says you're not allowed to see Nan."

"Kyren says, he'll kill you, if you crawl back to Gail again."

And so on.

I start to click out, drift away, when Mum goes on and on like that. I think up a song, it hardly has a tune, or a beat, but it works like that game we used to play at school, when we were really little:

> *"Kyren says, put your hands on your head,*
> *Kyren says shut your mouth,*
> *Kyren says you will end up dead,*
> *Kyren says no speaking out."*

When they're both in the flat, we stay in the corner. I sit at the table. Chloë stays in her buggy, facing me, not them. I feed her the school dinner scraps that I store in my blazer pockets. She used to stretch and screech to come out, the first few evenings, but now she stays

131

quiet. She knows not to bother speaking out.

Each morning, I wake up early. My eyes just ping open, without an alarm. I unplug my phone, really slowly, so it doesn't make a noise. And I pray Nan will keep paying my phone bill.

Chloë's usually still asleep in her buggy and we wheel quietly out. I close the front door - the absolute slowest you can imagine a person doing anything. I try so hard to avoid the clicks and clunks. But he always wakes on that final click shut and shouts from his bed, "See you soon, little pig."

The big, badman wolf.

I get us out of there and into the cold, dark start of the day. We walk and walk. I don't go back to that posh park again, in case we see Jen and her master.

I picture Shannon and Tommy and Derren – and all the other normal teenagers – still asleep. Normal teenagers are supposed to sleep a lot.

At nursery, a girl who works there - who is not much older than me - starts slipping a few nappies in Chloë's bag, at the end of each day. She is always the one who hands the bag to me.

I write on a piece of paper, "Thank you." I scrunch the thank you up, in the girl's hand, during a pick-up time. Then I wheel quickly away with Chloë.

The girl starts adding a couple of biscuits as well. When that happens, I wait until Chloë's asleep and don't share the biscuits with her. I feel so guilty, but I'm hungry.

I'm too hungry at the weekends especially - when Chloë eats nearly out-of-date jars of baby food, which I buy from the shop, with the money Nan gave me.

I wait for Mum and him to go to bed, before I can eat scraps of takeaway that they don't want. I don't dare spend any of that cash from Nan on myself.

Once, I'm starving so bad, I eat three slices of out-of-date bread, from a loaf in the flat. The next day, Mum notices there are less slices in the bag. She tells him. He bends my arm up my back, as he growls into my ear:

"You greedy, little pig."

After that, I can't hold my pen properly at school, for days.

I keep one eye open at night, so I'm beyond tired in the day. A few times, I've fallen asleep in lessons at school, but I've learned to cover it. I position myself to snooze in the corner. I work out which teachers never look up. I doze, when I'm sent to work in isolation.

I get bad marks and lunchtime stay-ins. Stuff that never happened to me, before I was Baby Girl.

I don't try to change their minds, though. Let me just be what they think I am. I have to use my energy to keep Chloë and me alive. And at least no adults noticing, means no adults asking questions - which means Chloë and me stay together.

I still play nursery rhymes for Chloë on my phone - when we're walking the pavements early morning, or if Mum and him both go out at night.

She likes Round and Round the Garden now. I sing her the proper version, but I've got my own twist too:

> *"Round and round each morning,*
> *Walking the same, dark streets,*
> *One step, two step,*
> *Dark words, hard lyrics, sad beats."*

CHAPTER 13

One Sunday, he's out drinking. Mum's in their room – she stays there mostly, when he's not around. So I let Chloë play out of her buggy.

I clear a space, moving the filth and the litter. I put some cushions round the edges and place Chloë down, where she can safely roll and pull herself about. She's happy rolling and I'm happy watching her. A wriggly, little worm.

Then the front door clangs. I tense up. Chloë looks towards the sound, scared - even little she is starting to know exactly what that front door clang means. As Mum flies out of her room to greet him, a quick lyric comes to me:

> *"No longer a doggy in the window,*
> *She's happy, yappy, greeting her male,*

135

Woof woof."

He's back from his Sunday drinking, with cans and a greasy takeaway. He stands in the hall, swaying, taking off his big, badman wolf coat. The smell of an afternoon of puffing, drinking and sniffing is rolling from him.

I deeply regret that I am in his chair - in his eye line - and that Chloë is also not in her buggy and not in my arms, or right next to me. But it's too late to move.

He comes to the doorway, "Having fun, are ya? Little piggies!" He laughs his laugh. "Oink, oink," he snorts, amusing himself. He licks his lips and runs his yellowing tongue over his sharp teeth. Mum has padded into the lounge, ears up, tail wagging.

"You okay, babe?" She says. Watching them, I hear another lyric, to the next part of How Much is that Doggy in the Window:

> *"He leaves her all day, staring out the window,*
> *She still calls him, 'Babes',*
> *Wags her tail,*
> *Woof, woof."*

He holds his coat out, for Mum to take. Then he grabs her face, in one of his big hands. He holds her tightly, round her jaw - it looks painful. He kisses her on the lips. Chloë is watching them. It makes me feel sick, that she can see all this.

They're distracted, so I move to scoop Chloë up, get her out of his way. But he flicks his head towards us, lips pulled back, sharp teeth on display.

"Leave her," he growls, in his no-messing voice.

I know, if he gets too angry in this sort of state, Chloë and me are in big danger. I stand still.

He sits. Puts the TV on. A big, badman wolf in a tracksuit, scoffing his takeaway, giving sportswear a bad name.

His eyes are glazed. He's necking cans. Guzzling. Burping. He doesn't offer Mum any of it.

She sits on the arm of his chair, sort of draped round the back of him. She's trying to look relaxed and in love, but her eyes keep twitching to Chloë, whenever the baby moves around the carpet. I don't know if it's because she's nervous for Chloë, or jealous of her.

Chloë is trying to pull herself to sitting. She keeps failing and trying, failing and trying. It's unreal, watching her trying to grow up, in the middle of this horror story. She belongs in a fairy tale cottage.

It looks like Chloë might manage it, like she might sit up, Then, she flops suddenly backwards, knocking her head with a bump on the floor. I wince for her. I think she'll suck it up, be okay, but, when she sees me flinch, she realises she's hurt herself. And then she starts to cry.

Mum's twitching on the armrest.

"Shut her up," he snarls at me. I move forward to pick Chloë up.

"No," he says, putting out a foot, his thick leg barring my way. "I said shut her up, not pick her up."

That makes it worse. Because I was coming for her and now I've stopped, Chloë gets more sad and turns up the volume on her crying.

He doesn't move. I look at his leg there, blocking my way. I could step, or jump, across it, but that would mean I'm starting a fight.

"Shut her up, now, " he says, growling louder. I don't know what to do. Chloë is now outraged that I'm not going to her. She's crying at max levels, like a dial on the mixing decks staying in the red.

If he won't let me go to her, there's only one other thing I can do, one thing I can try, to calm her down. I scroll quickly through the playlist in my mind and pick one I know she loves. I sing across the room to her:

> *"Round and round the garden,*
> *Like a teddy bear,*
> *One step, two step,*
> *Tickly under there."*

Chloë snivels and sobs still, but more slowly, watching me through the tears on her lashes. We lock our eyes on each other. I carry on, acting out the movements of the song on my hand, so she can see them:

> *"Round and round the haystack,*
> *Like a little mouse,*
> *One step, two step,*
> *Tickly in his house."*

Chloë stops crying. Her face is blotchy. Her eyes are wet. She becomes still and quiet. She seems so little and so very far away from me. I wish I could go to her.

A low, pounding laugh starts up, rolling out at us, from the big, badman wolf's belly:

"Ha, ha, ha, ha, ha, ha, ha."

Over and over again.

Shut up, I want to say.

Stop laughing, I want to say.

Chloë is looking from me, to him, to me. Her lip wobbles again. She's going to go any minute, so I carry on, into the third verse of the original:

"Round and round the lighthouse,
And up the spiral stair,
One step, two step,
We're right up in the air."

Chloë watches my hand, as I point towards the ceiling, in time with the end of the song.

He is still laughing, like a bad backing track that I'm trying to ignore. Mum's scornful voice comes in, like a cheap, harsh snare drum, from a low-skills producer:

"Hee, hee, hee."

"Ha, ha, ha, ha," he carries on. I feel the bass vibration of his laugh. It rattles through the floor and reaches my legs.

"Hee, hee, hee," Mum goes.

"Ha, ha, ha, ha," he goes.

I'd like to point at Mum and MC a lyric, to the beat of their laughing track:

"You're just a doggy in a window."

But I don't.

Instead, I smile at Chloë, who is looking very unsure, like she wants to stop crying and doesn't want to stop crying all at the same time. Chloë manages a little smile back, but she looks at Mum and him again, laughing, and her smile drops - she knows their laughter is not kind laughter.

Eventually, he stops laughing and asks Mum, "Did you teach her that song?

"As if, babe," Mum shakes her head.

Mum? Singing me a nursery rhyme? I wish I could laugh out loud at that one.

What next? It's like we're sitting in a gap,

between two tracks in a set list. What kind of beat is going to come on now? Me and Chloë don't get to decide that part.

He stands. He walks out of the living room, pulling up his joggers. "Let's go," he says to Mum, taking her by the wrist, as she stands too. They go next door to their room.

Enough time passes and I know they're not coming out. I swoop to get Chloë. I hold her tight, so tight I have to stop, because I might squeeze her too hard.

I open the front door quietly, leaving it on the latch. I stand on the walkway, Chloë to my chest, inhaling fresh and cold night air. I could not have taken one more breath in there, without choking.

Chloë relaxes onto my shoulder, as I sing to her:

> *"Round and round our days we go,*
> *We're quiet teddy bears,*
> *Some days we escape for a while,*
> *Then one step, two step, back here."*

CHAPTER 14

He's really paying attention to us now.

We're not just in the corner anymore, blending in with the shadows. We are no longer background to him, like dirt and cobwebs. He's watching us, targeting us. He'll zoom in on us, more and more. I know that about him.

I think about it, all day at school – Chloë and me, lost in a dark, dirty wood, with a big, badman wolf stalking us.

I walk slowly to collect Chloë from nursery – I want to see her, but I don't want to take her back, to that flat. I wait and play with her at The Lowdown, until nursery is all packed away and the room is ready for evening activities.

That's when I realise, today is Tuesday –

Hold the Mic day. I hear her, before I see her:

"Missie?"

I look up. Gail Force is shining bright like a diamond still. All gold hoops, big hair and white trackie, with the three stripes in gold too. Gail comes towards me in a clear, straight line. Then she sits on the floor with me and Chloë, like it doesn't matter if her white tracksuit gets marked.

"Where've you been?" Gail asks me, trying to catch my eye.

I avoid Gail's kind eyes. I look at the floor. Gail is still waiting for an answer.

I want to cry and be comforted by her, like I comfort Chloë, but I know I have to stay still and calm and keep my mouth shut.

So I shrug.

And I hate myself for it. For being like Mum. For having no other way to communicate.

Chloë has crawled over to see Gail and is pulling herself up on Gail's white trackie trousers. "Chloë, don't," I say, gently pushing her back.

"It's okay," Gail says to me, her voice like warmth from a radiator in winter.

"Hello, sweetheart," Gail says to Chloë. Chloë smiles and Gail Force tickles her chin. Chloë grins.

"Can I?" Gail opens her hands out to Chloë, but looks at me, waiting for permission to hold my baby. Fighting back the genetic shrug in me, I nod.

Gail holds Chloë, so Chloë is standing on Gail's lap. They look good together. Gail holds Chloë's arms up high, to help Chloë stand. While I am watching them, I feel so happy, because Gail is being kind to my baby. I feel tears come.

I look back down at the floor. I yawn to cover my tears, wiping my eyes at the same time. I have to keep Gail away from the idea that there's anything wrong. To keep me and Chloë safe. To keep us together.

If Gail has spotted my tears, she doesn't let on. Instead, she asks me, "Cuppa tea?"

I hate tea, but I nod - anything to distract Gail from the fact that I am crying. Gail carries Chloë ahead of me and leads the way to The Lowdown kitchen, which gives me more time to wipe the last tears away, breathe deep and get a happy face on.

Gail gets out the refreshments - tea bags, coffee, sugar, milk, squash, crisps, biscuits - all while holding Chloë on her hip. It's a feast that makes my tummy rumble - I haven't eaten yet at all today.

Gail wrestles with the big kettle, still holding Chloë. The clanging sounds, as Gail fills the kettle with water and places it down, remind me of summers in the park with the steel drum band.

Me and Shannon used to dance with our dancing school. Derren, and some of the other kids from school, would play as part of the band. We'd have summer park open days - we don't anymore.

The memory makes me a feel like a little girl, when I need to act like an adult. I focus on today.

I listen to the tin drum kettle warming, crunching and creaking its slow way to boiling.

Sqwoooossssh, sqwaasssh.

But those sad tears are still simmering in me. Trying to rise back up.

Gail Force clatters and bangs about, getting everything ready. I concentrate on the beat from the kettle drum, listening as it clicks and clacks. I'm acting calm on the outside and working like mad on the inside - I have to think hard, so I don't let it all out and break down.

Kettle, beats, lyrics. Gail puts a sweet, milky tea in front of me. Polly Put the Kettle On lyrics start to bubble in my head:

> *"Gail Force put the kettle on,*
> *Big kettle on,*
> *Like an old steel drum,*
> *Gail Force put the kettle on,*
> *Now tears,*
> *You must go away."*

It's such a silly thing to think, a mad song to write. I laugh out loud, then stop the laugh, as soon as it rises up, so it ends up sounding like a bark meeting a hiccup.

But Gail knows I'm laughing. She grins and asks me, "What's so funny?"

I don't answer. How could I ever explain the picture in my head? I want to shrug, but I really don't want to shrug, so I sip the tea Gail's given me, to distract myself. I concentrate on the tea. It tastes good. It tastes sugary and milky.

Gail is holding Chloë, leaning back against the opposite kitchen counter and watching me drinking. "Where've you been?" Gail asks again.

I don't want to shrug. I don't want to be rude. And I don't want to lie. So, I speak something of the truth:

"My mum came for us. We're living with her." I sip my tea again.

Gail Force shakes her head - not at me, but like she's disagreeing with herself. She opens a chocolate chip cookie pack. "Can I give Chloë one?" Gail asks me. I've never been asked for so much permission.

I nod.

Gail passes Chloë a cookie, which Chloë is delighted about. Gail then offers the packet to me. I carefully take a cookie, when I want to grab and scoff the whole pack. I nibble it, like it's no big deal, trying to show I have manners.

It tastes incredible. I haven't had a chocolate chip cookie in forever. It's gone in two bites. Gail puts five cookies on a plate and puts them down next to me.

I eat. Chloë crunches. Gail sips her tea. For a while, the three of us munch, or sip. Then

Gail speaks:

"Badman."

I stop crunching the last cookie, holding my mouth still, full of crumbs. Gail has the same name for him as I do?

"He's always been a badman," Gail says. I look up. Gail is brushing bits of cookie from Chloë's chin. Chloë pats Gail's face, as if to say thank you.

Gail gives me Chloë back. She starts moving stuff around in the kitchen, setting up the things she's already set up, like she's keeping herself busy.

I'm glad Gail's thought of something to do, because the kettle's stopped whooshing and swooshing - and I've run out of ways to distract myself, to stop the sadness coming out.

There's no lyrics in my head. There's no beat to write a song to.

The front door to The Lowdown bangs shut, down the corridor. Voices. People arriving for Hold the Mic. I can hear their normal teenager chatter, as they start to fill the building.

Gail pops her head out and says hello, asks them to set the chairs up. It's time for

Chloë and me to go. To head back out into our daily round and round.

Gail returns to the kitchen. She unlocks the hatch that opens up to the main room. Gail's DJ must have come quietly in, while we've been drinking tea. The speaker is humming - the power is on, but there no beats yet. The coloured lights are sequencing.

I would love to stay here tonight, to listen to music, to be around people who don't want to hurt me.

Gail Force is looking out at the room, but she speaks back to me:

"Are you coming tonight?"

I want to. I might get back to the flat, as I often do, and find that they're out, or asleep. Then Chloë and I will have to wait for ages, in the cold dark, for someone to let us in.

When we could have been here instead.

The DJ sets the microphone on its stand - it sparkles in many colours, from the lights. It twinkles, like a star.

I can't stop looking at it.

Gail asks me again, "You gonna come?"

I put my tea down and hitch my baby up.

"Yes," I say. "I'm coming to Hold the Mic."

CHAPTER 15

I'm pretending.

I'm a normal teenager.

I walk into the main room of The Lowdown, returning to Hold the Mic night, like any other normal teenager, who took a break for a few weeks.

I see groups of people. I see Shannon, Tommy, Derren – they're near the front of the room, in a huddle, with a couple of other people I don't know.

Everyone else here looks free, light, happy.

The weight of my baby on my hip and the sadness in my heart, remind me that I'm kidding myself, if I think I can be normal like them.

I think about turning back. But Gail Force is behind me, so I keep moving forward.

Gail Force gets a chair and sits in the middle, at the front. People grab chairs also, moving towards Gail, like they know how she wants them to sit. Are they making a circle? I don't dare pick up a chair and make a space for myself among them. I stop.

Gail waves me over. She points to a chair next to her, which makes everyone look and see me. I stare at Chloë, to avoid their stares. The colours of the DJ's lights sprinkle on Chloë's face, like a magic spell. She smiles. She kicks her legs against my hip. She looks happy, at least. She looks comfortable, for the first time in ages. How Chloë feels gives me courage to take one step, two step.

The others have spotted me. By the time I get to the chair next to Gail, Shannon has rushed to grab the chair next to me. Shannon grins and looks so happy to see us. Chloë smiles and flaps about – she has always loved Shannon.

As the group settles, I feel grateful for the half-darkness. Everyone else is here in their night time clothes. Things they choose to wear –

hi-tops, pumps, big winter boots, puffa coats, rain jackets, hoodies, jeans, joggers, trackie tops.

And I am wearing my school uniform - and a dirty uniform at that. I sink low in my seat, Chloë on my lap, so she's looking at out everyone, while also hiding me. They all grin and wave at her - I'm relieved to be holding the world's cutest distraction.

Chloë's got Shannon's little finger in her hand, trying to put it in her mouth. Shannon leans back and whispers to me, "It's so good to see you." I want to run away and hide, but I owe Shannon some of my words. I whisper to her:

"I'm sorry I didn't return your messages and that."

I breathe slowly – it takes something from me, to say that to her. I feel myself wobble, in the place where tears spring from.

"Don't be daft," Shannon nudges me. Then she grins, "I'm just glad you're back. Now, you can show them how a real MC holds the mic."

It feels good to be near Shannon. To be close to her hair products and her lotions. Her kindness. I feel so bad for the way my life has made me treat her. Who would want to be best friends with me?

I start to sink into my sadness. I wonder how different I am from Mum and Nan, if I think it's alright to pick up and drop people? It's what I did to Shannon and it's what they do to me. But I don't have time to dwell, because Gail signals to the DJ and he starts a beat.

Gail gets up and takes the mic. She makes hand signals to the DJ, for him to push the tempo and wind to a different part of the track. Most people are watching the way Gail and the DJ are in synch, waiting for Gail to start performing. But, I realise, a few are watching Chloë too. She's flapping her little duck feet to the rhythm and she's perfectly in time with the beat.

Gail holds the mic to the side of her mouth and begins:

> "It's Tuesday, say,
> Another Hold the Mic Day..."

Gail holds out the mic, as everyone else joins in for the "Hold the Mic day" part. She continues:

"Nothing bars the way,
To the words we came to say,
If you jump in, as he plays..."

Gail points to the DJ, then carries on:

"You've got to own yourself,
Be brave,
There's nothing shameful in mistakes..."

Gail holds the mic back out to the group and cups her other hand to her ear. Everyone, but me and Chloë, joins in:

"There'll be another chance,
Another week,
Another time,
For Hold the Mic day."

Everyone whoops. People stand and shake hands. They fist-bump and high-five each other. They look like they do this every week - I've missed so much, by not being able to come here.

I stay in my seat. Chloë is my shield. People approach and give her a little fist bump, or high-five. I can't look at anyone. I feel too ashamed of how I appear - how I look is how I live.

Everyone goes back to their seats. The beat continues to flow and blend into other tracks, at the hand of the DJ. I'm looking forward to sliding as far down in my seat as possible, for the rest of the session. And then to never coming here again.

But then Gail points at the DJ, who nods and flips the track to something bouncing, with a popping bass. People's toes are tapping, their shoulders are moving.

Gail speaks, "It's hold the mic time." Then she offers the mic out to the side, next to me. Chloë grabs for it and I reach out quickly, to save the mic from her dribbly fingers.

Now, I'm holding the mic first, at Hold the Mic. What happens next?

People are moving, smiling, waiting. Chloë is jigging up and down, which thankfully hides the fact my legs are shaking. I look at Shannon, ready to pass the mic straight on to her, but Shannon leans back, away from the mic. She smiles and nods at me, "Go on, Missie."

"Missie Misdemeanour everyone," Derren yells and beatboxes a siren sound. I think about how the flat is waiting for me, across the square, with the big, badman wolf inside it. This will be the only chance I get to come to Hold the Mic again. I know it.

I move the mic up, so Chloë can't grab it. I don't even know what's going to come out of my mouth yet. My brain is reading the beat. Playing for time, my voice shakes into the mic:

> *"One step,*
> *Two step,*
> *Jump into the beat right there."*

Gail Force nods to the beat. Shannon starts dancing in her seat. People are smiling and moving. Chloë wiggles on my knee.

The mic is shaking in my hand, but it's my one chance - I'll be back in his corner, in an hour or two. I go in:

> *"I came in here before,*
> *Gail Force said, stay,*
> *She put the kettle on,*
> *Little did she know,*

In my own head,
I made a song,
The sound the kettle screeched,
It made a beat,
It helped me write a song,
Now I freestyle to this track,
Straight off the bat,
I sing along."

I need to take a breath.

People clap, pump the air. Dare I look around the room, at them?

But I'm not finished yet. I wait, with the mic, at the edge of whatever I'm going to say next. I find a different section of the track, a part that's got a faster tempo.

I bounce my next lyrics over the top of the beat:

"I'm making this up,
I'm thinking out loud,
Got no thought ahead,
What's gonna come out,
Me and she walk around,
When you see us about,
Know bars in my head,

Are in my mind loud,
I can't make it stop,
Counting them out,
Patterns and tapping,
Count lyrics how,
So, I came back tonight,
And I hope she feels proud,
I'm a good teenage mum,
Let these words be allowed."

I get so lost in the lyrics, pour all of me into the mic, that I do not notice people on their feet, moving to my words, to the music I make with the DJ's track. They are dancing to the song I wrote in front of them.

Shannon is on her feet, as is Derren. Even Tommy is head-nodding, leg-shuffling in his seat. I've sent out all this energy to people. I can't believe it. Gail gently takes the mic from me. "Does anyone want to follow that?" Gail says. She holds the mic out to the circle.

"Hell, no," they all reply. Gail speaks again:

"I said, does anyone want to follow that?"

"Hell no," goes the reply again. It's

another one of those Hold the Mic things, I think. Something they all know how to do, except me. I don't mind it this time, though. I can see they're all being kind. I breathe out.

Gail turns to me. She holds her free hand to her heart and locks eyes with me. She speaks into the mic:

"It's Missie - this week's Hold the Mic winner, everyone!"

There's lots more cheering. The DJ plays a big, bassy track and the lights flash more rapidly. People come over to us again. I nod at them. I feel kind of good right now.

I think about those magic wishes I wanted. I wish we could stay here, at Hold the Mic, for all of the rest of our days.

I sit back in my seat. The energy rush from performing has left me shaking. I can't hold myself up. I look at the floor - the lights are dancing upon it.

But then I feel time pass, flow on - the world leaves me behind, like always. I was only normal for the shortest of times.

Soon, it's refreshments. I feel so weak with separation from everything, that I pass Chloë to Shannon and walk quickly to the loo. I wait there, under the cold, bright light, hiding in a cubicle, until I hear everyone go back after break time.

I've used all my energy, holding the mic in front of everyone, making up that song. And, now that we're in the second half of Hold the Mic, I'm just thinking about how me and Chloë have got to go back to that flat.

Gail is checking her watch. Time's up. We're leaving. I've been hiding in The Lowdown for hours. But it's time to return to the big, badman wolf. Shannon's put Chloë in her buggy for me. Chloë looks tired – she's got her thumb in her mouth.

Gail walks across the room with me, keeping to one side of Chloë's buggy. "You gonna be alright?" Gail whispers, as Shannon links my arm on the other side.

I nod - what else can I do?

"You lot are walking home together?" Gail asks. I realise Tommy and Derren are also keeping pace with us.

"Yes, ma'am," Derren replies, stopping to salute, like an American soldier in a film.

Gail holds the outside door open. The lads aren't even at the bottom of the path tonight. Everyone respects Gail round here, it seems – except the people I have to live with.

I leave, with my friends. I want to say goodbye. I want to say thank you to Gail. But I can't.

"See you next week," Gail says.

"See you next week," Shannon calls.

"See you never," I think, as we go.

We walk home. I'm wheeling Chloë to hell, while my friends chat about normal teenager stuff. Me and Chloë are sliding down the waterspout, to a soundtrack of meaningless conversation about box sets, music, DJs and weekend plans.

I want to take back every other wish I ever thought of making.

I only have one wish right now:

I wish the outside light to the flat was off.

CHAPTER 16

I see her, before I even see the light outside his flat, which is on, of course.

Mum is out on the walkway. She paces. She is looking, smoking, waiting. She leans over the wall and screeches at me:

"Where've you been?!"

I've come to a stop. And so have my friends.

"Get up here now!" Mum's eyes are popping out of her head. The attack dog is straining at her chains. She wants to pounce. She's so wound up, she could lash out at anyone.

I need to get my friends out of here. They don't deserve to be dragged into this.

I step away from Shannon. I don't want to, but I must. And then I do the next thing I know I have to do.

I leave Chloë behind me.

I can't take her in there tonight. I've broken his rule. I'm going to be punished. I can tell from the state Mum is in, that he must be beyond angry. I'm going to save Chloë from what's coming.

If I look back at my baby girl now, I will never be able to leave her.

"Missie!" Shannon calls, her voice sounds as tight and scared, as I feel inside. The boys are waiting, really near me, as if they might step forward to stop me, to try to help. No. I wave my arm, shoo them away.

As I place one foot at the bottom of the stairwell, I can hear Shannon's feet pit-pat fast towards me. She pulls on my arm. Not linking, but insisting. And she is strong, from all the dancing and sports.

I can hear Mum shouting foul words about me and heading along the walkway, to the top of the stairs. I have to get Chloë gone, far away from what's coming.

I look at Shannon. "Please," I say.

Shannon's eyes are huge, with fear and worry. She grips my arm tighter.

"Don't make me come down there!" Mum yells down the stairwell. I look to Mum, to Shannon, to Chloë.

"Let's tell my mum," says Shannon, leaning back with the effort of trying to get me to leave with her. "We can't keep it all a secret any longer."

No. It's too late for telling anyone anything. If I run now, he will be one-step, two-steps behind us. Then Shannon will pay, maybe her mum, and Chloë definitely will.

He will hurt us all, smash up the place. It's better that it's just me. Plus, there's only Shannon I can trust with my baby, so she has to go away with her.

"Take her," I say to Shannon. "Please."

"Missie!" Mum's shriek bounces off the stone of the stairwell. I hear her angry footsteps heading down the stairs.

Shannon looks unsure. Is she going to crumble?

I look at the boys. At Derren. I know he knows how to look after children - how to be a good uncle.

"Derren, please," I say to him. Derren nods and crosses to the buggy. Mum's slippers are slapping down the stone stairs – one more flight of steps, until she reaches me.

"Run to yours with her," I whisper to Shannon. "Fast."

I feel a different kind of arm link through mine now. Bony, sharp, furious. It's Mum. Her teeth are bared, the twists and knots of her neck muscles stick out.

Mum's dragging me, pulling me, up the stairs. On the second flight, I see my friends and hear Chloë's buggy wheels rattle-clatter, as they run for it. Go, I think. One run, two run.

I see people opening the doors to their flats. Letting their light into the night, as they peep outside, wondering what's going on.

The flat door is open - Mum pulls me through it.

"Where've you been?" She screams, hitting my head. I curl up, cover myself. Then I hear him speak:

"Close the door."

I hear the front door click.

"Ask her again," he growls. I'm still curled up tight, but I can tell he's close and moving closer. Mum's chopping down on my back and my arms. She yells, high-pitched, into my ear:

"Where've you been? Where've you been?"

Over and over.

Eventually, she runs out of breath and has to stop. I hear her panting - still that doggy in a window:

"Woof, woof."

I hear him take one step, two step. He pulls my head up, yanking me by the hair. He holds his face close to mine.

My, my, what big teeth he has - the big, badman wolf.

"Answer her," he snarls. Mum hits me once, really hard, round the back of my head - I bite my tongue, with the impact.

"Say it!" Mum screams. I know I have to try and fight to save myself, so I make something up:

"I've been for a walk." My voice sounds small, shrivelled. To think earlier tonight, I held a mic that no one else dared touch, after I'd spoken into it.

"I told you she'd lie," Mum says.

His chest lifts. He widens his shoulders.

Big, badman wolf.

"Where've you been?" His voice is so deep now, I feel the growling bass of it, through my body, like a sickness I can't stop coming.

"I've been for a walk," I cry. I'm too scared now, to be able to cover it. I feel him rock back, ready to pounce.

I know how this story ends, but still I try for a different ending anyway - I turn and cower, as if I'm flinching from the coming attack, but then I leap forward. I reach for the door.

I get my hand on the latch.

I hear him yell, "Get hold of her!" I feel Mum's bony hand make a grab for me, but my school uniform is slippy in Mum's grip and I slide free.

My hands are shaking, but I tell myself, get the door open.

And I do.

I feel the cold air of the night on my face.

My last chance.

I get one foot out on the walkway.

There's a woman outside her flat, looking down towards us, hugging her dressing gown around herself. I shout, "Help me!"

But then he's got me.

I'm pulled back.

I feel my feet leave the floor. My body flies through the air and lands, smack, against the shelf in the hall.

Something in my back cracks.

The big, badman wolf is looming over me. I don't even have a straw house, like the worst-off little pig, for just a moment of protection.

All I've got now, is wherever I can send myself in my mind.

"Shut that front door and keep it shut," he says to Mum. She scampers to close the door, locks it, hurries back.

Woof, woof, I think. Yes, that's it. It's all I have. My mind. Let me compose a lyric:

> *"How much is that good doggy on the walkway?*
> *He shouts and she says three bags full,*
> *Woof, woof,*
> *She sits, pants, begs, does whatever he*

says..."

As the lyrics flow through my mind, I get dragged, by the neck of my school jumper. The skin on my legs burns, as I'm pulled across the floor and into the lounge. I am thrown on to my front, in the middle of the room.

I can see all the filth, the food and the cigarette ends, on the floor. Is the spider in its web, in the kitchen corner? I would love to see her right now, if she is.

I move my head, to try and look for Incy Wincy.

"Forget it," the Wolf growls, as he places a foot on my back, pinning me to the ground, pressing on all the soft parts and the small bones in me - bits not designed to be pressed on.

I feel things crack and crunch, click and strain, with the pressure.

I feel the sole of the Wolf's shoes, pinching my skin, as he pushes more and more of his weight, through his foot, onto me. He speaks:

"One... More... Time..."

The Wolf's deep voice is rumbling

through his foot and into the middle of me. "Where've you been?"

"Tell the truth, Missie," Mum barks, standing nearby – good doggy. She should get a biscuit for this.

I can't tell the truth to these two. I have to try to lie my way to not getting a full beating, or worse:

"Chloë wouldn't stop crying."

The Wolf presses yet more weight into my back. I wish so much that I could see Incy Wincy – my only friend here.

Something soft, in my stomach, gets hot and tight, like it might pop. But I have to keep trying, keep lying - like Incy Wincy would keep climbing:

"I took Chloë out, to get her to go to sleep."

Bad move. He'd not realised before, but now the Wolf catches on to the fact that Chloë's not here. "Where is she now?" The Wolf demands. I feel air rush towards me, as his boot makes contact with my side.

"Missie's left her with her friends," Mum says. Yap, yap, sit and beg. I wish Mum would curl up in her dog basket and die.

"Go and get her, then," he barks at Mum.
No, please.

I have to distract him, stop him sending his attack dog, to bring Chloë back here. Mum will carry my sweet girl to the Wolf, in her jaws.

"I..." I can't breathe. His foot is pressing the air from my chest. I push the words out:

"I went to Hold the Mic."

The Wolf pulls me up from the floor. He throws me again. I land hard, on the sofa. Something splits with a bang – I don't know if it's me, or the furniture.

The Wolf fills the room, roaring, spittle flying, "Think you can be an MC, do ya?" I can't speak to reply.

"Answer me!" The Wolf shouts.

"Babe," yaps the Good Doggy. "Someone's gonna hear you." The Wolf lunges for Good Doggy and puts it out, in its room, slamming the bedroom door shut.

While he's out there, my phone rings. I move through the pain of many things bust and broken in me, to get it from my pocket. Shannon. I accept the call, as I hear the Wolf pound back in.

The Good Doggy is whimpering and

scratching at the bedroom door, but she doesn't try to come out. "Babe," the Good Doggy whines. "Babe, don't do it." Over and over.

Where's Incy Wincy, I think? The Wolf is almost upon me.

I look across to the kitchen, catch one glimpse of the web of the spider, covered in dust. She's in the dirty, dark hell of this place, and yet she's still clinging, climbing, spinning, for her life.

I have time to see that the call to Shannon is still open, on my phone.

And then he's got me and all I can do now to get through this, is think of lyrics:

> *"Incy Baby Girl Spider,*
> *Climb up the waterspout.*
> *Straight after all this, Incy my girl,*
> *You and Chloë are going to climb out,*
> *You two are going to survive this,*
> *See sunshine after the rain,*
> *Pain's passing,*
> *Means nothing,*
> *You can do it,*
> *Lock yourself in,*
> *Baby Girl,*

Get through the pain."

He is really hurting me now.

I need more to cling to. I think of Hold the Mic. All the people smiling, fist-pumping. I remember how the microphone felt like it was part of me.

I repeat the verse in my mind:

"Incy Baby Girl Spider..."

As the pain builds, I have to also build the Hold the Mic memory up in my mind, focus on it more. I add a stage, lights shining on me, the glint of a microphone stand.

When it gets so I'm hardly here anymore, there's one line, like a track skipping back again. Looping. All I have left is:

> *"You and Chloë are going to climb out,*
> *"You and Chloë are going to climb out,*
> *"You and Chloë are going to climb out..."*

And then the flat front door goes bang, slam, crash – it flies open. I see the Wolf panic, shrink.

Feet crash in, loud voices shout:

"Where is she?"

Mum comes - yap, yap - out of her room. "Get out!" Yap, yap, yap. "Get out! You can't just bust in!"

The Wolf is hiding behind the sofa.

Lights, people, a real dog, fly into the room. The dog barks, loud, and leaps for the Wolf.

"She's in here," someone shouts. I feel people round me.

Someone else says, "She's alive, boss."

"Chloë?" I ask.

I feel like someone is fading me out, like I'm the end of a song.

The last thing I see is that cobweb.

"Me and Chloë are going to climb out," I say.

CHAPTER 17

I'm in the real world briefly, then back out.

I'm asleep, then I'm awake, then I'm asleep - but feeling like I'm awake and vice versa.

I'm alone, then crowded by people. They're wearing uniforms, all different kinds, or their own normal clothes. They prod me, test me, shine lights in my eyes, talk about me.

For days.

Eventually, I'm awake for longer than I'm asleep. That's when I realise, I'm still alive.

Then, the day after that, there are people. Gail Force, two plain clothes police, a social worker called Sandra. Nan.

They are waiting on chairs, around the edges of a room, where I'm lying in a bed that's high up from the floor.

I act like I'm still waking up, so I can assess this situation, before they all start assessing me.

I've been in something like this before – when Chloë was born.

Social workers and the police wanted to know how she got there. I said nothing.

I was visited by Mum, the night after Chloë came. She told me he would kill everyone - her, Nan, the baby, me (she put us in that order). She told me I had to keep us all safe.

Mum was the first to say, what he later said to me so many times. Whenever he saw me, it was:

"Keep your mouth shut."

And that is what I have done.

But then it was only about me. Now, I have my baby girl and she is not living like this. I have to do something about it. I'm alive to fight for her, when I didn't know if I would be. Now, I have to stay alive.

In the hospital room, I look at Nan, who is staring at the floor. Where've you been, Nan? Where were you, when me and Chloë needed you? Why didn't you visit us? Or try to help us, when we were in his flat?

I wish Nan would get out. Leave. Why is she even here now? The plain-clothes policewoman speaks:

"Missie?"

I look at her. She is Mum's age, I think, but like a normal version of that age – tidy hair, nice face, good teeth. The policewoman speaks again:

"We've come to hear your story."

Nan interrupts, speaking quickly over the policewoman, "Missie…"

Nan's tone means, listen to me. Nan is staring at me, wanting me to make eye contact. But I don't.

"No more secrets, Nan," I say, looking at the ceiling, so I can avoid the hidden meaning in Nan's eyes.

I'm going to do this, tell everyone, but I have something I need to know first:

"Where's my baby?"

Social Sandra answers me, "She's in temporary foster care."

"You let them take her away?" I shout at Nan. The shout comes out of me like a roar. It shocks me - I've never shouted at Nan before.

Nan looks at the floor.

"Answer me, Nan!" I shout even louder. I need to know why Nan has walked away from Chloë, when Chloë needed her. I remember Nan leaving us at the bottom of the steps to his walkway, to go up alone to his flat.

"Why Nan?" I say, more quiet - the shout has hurt my voice and I feel silly shouting now, with everyone watching.

Nan shakes her head.

Then, Nan shrugs - just like Mum would.

Nan shrugs off Chloë and shrugs off me. The family shrug - is Nan the creator of it, or does it go even further back than her?

Social Sandra says, "Chloë is safe and being well looked after." The policewoman sits forward. I can see her badge - her name's Jemilah. She has light tan skin. She looks a bit like me - it makes me think I can tell my secrets to her. Jemilah speaks:

"Let us help you. We all want to keep you safe."

"She doesn't," I say, pointing at Nan. Nan looks up.

"How can you say that?" Nan says, shaking her head and looking at the others, like they're already on her side.

But no one responds.

"How could you let them take her?" I ask Nan. Nan doesn't answer.

"How could you let Mum take us there?" I'm shouting again now, even though my throat is hurting with each word that comes out.

Nan is shaking her head to herself and picking up her bag. She's getting ready to go, turn, walk away, like she did before.

And that's when I can't control myself. Two more words fly out of me, like a scream:

"You knew!"

I only really understand what I mean, once I've said it out loud. Yes, Nan has always known what happened to me, how Chloë came. She just didn't want to do anything about it.

Nan stands up. She points at me, "You're a piece of work, you are, Missie. All the time and effort I've put into you. How can you be so ungrateful?"

Nan is pulling her coat round herself. Her face is tight and angry. "I'm not staying here, to be spoken to like that," Nan says to the other adults in the room. Then she goes, scuttles out. Leaves me to it.

Gail tuts loudly, as Nan goes, but Nan ignores her. I can see shock on the other adults' faces. The room is quiet.

"She doesn't want me to speak," I say.

"Well, we do," Gail says - her voice is warm, where Nan's was cold. "We are here for it, aren't we?" Gail looks at the other adults and they all nod. Gail can lead even this room like a pro. It's as if we're at Hold the Mic and she's telling us what to do next.

I wish we were there - at Hold the Mic.

I wish I was with Chloë.

"Are you ready to talk to us?" Jemilah asks.

I'm not ready.

But telling my truth is the only I way I can make my wish to be with Chloë come true. I have to keep climbing up the waterspout for the both of us.

I hold the Incy Wincy rhythm in my mind. I think of the sunshine that I will feel upon me, once I get to the top.

I picture Chloë on purpose, like I am drawing her in my mind. Wispy hair, one fang gnawing on her travel cot.

Her legs are wobbling. Her chin is

covered in drool. She is smiling and waiting for a song from me. A song about an Incy Wincy Spider. The song of my life.

I begin:

> "Kyren, he's a big, badman wolf,
> He'd say, I can't go out,
> He'd power down upon us,
> He'd beat us and he'd shout,
> My mum would think it's all fine,
> She'd let him have his way,
> Then he knew he could do anything,
> And nobody would say."

I don't stop, keep going, the lyrics of my story tumbling out, to that Incy Wincy tune:

> "Nan knew he's a badman wolf,
> She knew he'd beat and shout,
> She'd never ask how Chloë came,
> But I think she worked it out,
> We stayed with her, the baby and me,
> At hers, at least we were safe,
> But then Mum said we had to go back,
> Since then, we've lived in chains."

I'm almost there, but the ending feels so far away. I don't know if I can get to it. I don't want to relive it.

No, don't stop.

Keep scrabbling. Keep telling them:

"I tried not to anger the wolf,
I tried to keep myself small,
But he would get mad, and stomp and bang,
He threw me against the wall,
The night I stayed for Hold the Mic,
He went back on the attack,
He battered, and shattered and broke me,
I thought I was done, that was that."

I stop. Everything is silent. No one is moving in the hospital room. I realise I am breathing hard and my throat is so sore, with the effort of speaking. I have a few words left in me - they are so important, but I have hardly any battery remaining to say them. I think I whisper them, though they feel so loud:

"It was him."

CHAPTER 18

My wish isn't coming true. I'm alone here, in this darkening waterspout.

I imagine Chloë is in her travel cot, an angel sleeping, next to me. Her little chest rising and falling, so I know she's alive. But when I turn, hoping she will actually be there, all I see is a shining, cold, hospital floor.

Wherever she is, is someone watching her? Is someone checking she's breathing, like I always do?

There's a movement in the doorway. It's Nan. She's back. Is she sorry? Is she going to make everything better at last?

She's hunched over, in shadow. I pull myself up to sitting, feeling my stitches and bruises, my internal injuries, my pain. "Nan?"

My voice sounds hopeful.

"Your mum wants to talk to you," Nan says.

Oh no, Nan. Why? Why, is it always Mum over me?

"Tell her, I don't want to," I say, forcing my voice out of me.

"Tell me yourself," Mum says.

I put my hand on the bed controller that is resting on the covers next to me. I use it to click the bedside light on.

Nan looks old. She looks untidy. Her eyes are dull. I predict wine has been drunk. Mum is standing a few steps behind Nan. Mum's scrawnier than ever, her tracksuit hanging from her.

I keep my fingers on the controller, which also has an alarm on – shall I press it and call the nurses?

Mum speaks to Nan, "Wait outside." Nan looks unsure.

Nan, don't leave. Don't.

"Please," I say to Nan.

Nan shrugs. "It's not up to me," she says, looking away, at the floor, avoiding my eyes.

"Just go," Mum says.

"Don't be long, love," Nan says, squeezing Mum's arm gently. "I'll wait outside."

I get it now. I really and completely understand something, for the first time. Nan is only here for Mum in this life. Nan can't see us – Chloë and me. And she sees Mum for something's she's not.

That's why I've always felt invisible.

No one's been looking.

I want Nan to know something, before she goes. I call after her, "You've left me alone for the last time, Nan."

Nan stops, keeping her back to me. I watch her body tense, as she hesitates. Is she going to come back in and make this all different?

She goes.

I'm alone with Mum.

The room feels small. Mum's at the foot of the bed. Her eyes are dark, like black glitter. Her mouth is shaped like she can taste something bad.

"Let's get your story straight," Mum says.

Her voice is deep and tired, full of long

nights - crying, drinking, smoking, shouting, yapping and everything else she does to herself.

I feel the alarm button in my hand.

Mum grips the bottom of the bed, her knuckles tight across the metal frame. I know I should press the button now. I can see from how tense Mum is, that she is seconds from doing harm to me. But I want to hear what she's got to say. I want to really see Mum as she is, instead of wishing about who she might be.

"What have you told them already?" Mum says. She wants to sound fierce – she thinks I am still a powerless, little girl. She thinks she's telling me not to make a fuss, like in the old days.

But I'm a mum now too – and I want to be good at it.

"What have you said?" Mum's getting impatient already. Her question tells me something important - something that gives me strength. I realise Mum and Nan have no idea what happened this afternoon, after Nan left me to it. They don't know what I said. They don't know how much everyone else knows.

At last, I have something that they don't. I have a secret they haven't made me keep.

Mum moves towards me, into the pool of brightness made by the bedside light. I watch her chew quickly, gnawing on her bitten-down nails.

The skin under Mum's eyes is dark blue and green - I can't tell if it's bruises, or tiredness. With her hair pulled back and her eyes wide, Mum looks like a skeleton.

"Tell me," Mum says. She's trying to sound scary, but I can hear she's desperate. She is inching towards me, rocking back a little, each time, before she creeps forwards once more. Shall I press the alarm button now?

I'll wait - Mum won't come for me, while she doesn't have an answer, while I have some power.

"Tell me what you've said," Mum hisses.

I decide to give Mum a dose of her own nasty medicine.

I shrug.

"What does that mean?" Mum's raising her voice. She catches herself, looking towards the window for a minute, like she's having a word with her reflection.

Is it herself that she sees mirrored back at her? Or, is it him? Is it her, speaking to me? Or, is it really him, in her head? Pulling her strings?

Mum sighs - her classic, disappointed, all-about- me sigh. I know all Mum's moves. I think ahead - what will Mum do next? Yes, here comes the manipulation, don't-make-a-fuss part.

Mum sits on the end of the bed.

"You don't want to break my heart, do you?" Mum says, trying to sound soft and sad - it reminds me of the voice Nan speaks to Mum with, when Nan's trying to keep Mum calm.

If I agree to what Mum wants now, she'll be kind to me for a minute. Maybe stroke my hair, like she used to. But it won't be because she loves me. It will be because I've done what she wanted. What he told her, what he wanted me to do.

I'm so sick of it all.

The way Mum and Nan and him have got everything twisted in my head. Since I was little. Since I was a baby. A baby like Chloë.

I know I could never treat Chloë the way Mum has treated me.

So, what do I do next? To break out of all this? Mum is in the room with me. I can't run from her - my body is too weak. I will have to use my mind to escape.

I ask Mum a question, throwing the next move to her, as I plot my escape route:

"Do you want me to lie?"

I feel Mum clench. She's quiet for a while. How can she answer me, without admitting what he's done? If she answers yes, he's guilty. If she answers no, I get to tell the truth.

Mum replies, "I want you to tell them what happened."

Wait.

Have I read this wrong? Does Mum understand after all?

I move my fingers slightly away from the alarm button, so I don't accidentally press it.

Mum leans over me. I see the stains of brown between her teeth - when she was my age, on her school photo, her teeth were so clean and shining.

"Tell them you attacked him," Mum says.

Oh.

I see.

How could I think anything else?

Mum carries on with her instructions, "Tell

them you wanted all this." Mum leans so close, her stale breath is hitting me in the face.

I'm ready to press that alarm button. But first, I'm going to claim my truth from her. This one time, I'm going to fight back.

"I already did, Mum," I say.

Mum looks at me, eyes narrowed, waiting to understand what I mean. I sit up a little bit, moving through the pain, the everywhere in me that hurts.

"I told them everything – the beatings, the fear, how Chloë came – all of it. This afternoon."

Mum lunges for me and I press the alarm.

CHAPTER 19

Mum shouts, "You've ruined my life!"

The bedside alarm sounds like beats on repeat:

> *"Beep, bleep,*
> *Bleep, beep."*

People rush in - more and more of them - trying to get hold of Mum. Get her out of the room. All the while, the:

> *"Beep, bleep,*
> *Bleep, beep."*

And Mum yelling lyrics over the beats:

"She's lying!
She's a liar!"

Nurses come. Then doctors, porters, security. Eventually, the police arrive too.

When they take Mum away, she is spitting, screaming. She is flailing, grabbing, popping and her arms, muscles, bones, her angry face – they make a picture that burns onto my mind and stays there, long after she's gone.

I hear Mum shouting to Nan, as Mum's voice is pulled further away down the corridor:

"Mum, tell them! Tell them it's all her fault. Tell them she wanted to."

I know Nan will be trying to soothe Mum, like she always does, saying things like, "Come on, darling... Calm down, Belle, love..."

I've seen it so many times before.

Nan doesn't come back in, to see if I'm okay.

The nurses, doctors, the on-call social worker – they all look at me with sad eyes. All these years, I've lived my truth silently, invisible, not sure if even I believed it. But now, I'm broken, bruised and in this bed. And everyone can see it's real – even me.

They've taken photos, they've operated on me. No one can deny what has happened to me. I don't even have to say it, except I do – if I want to be free of Mum and Nan and him forever.

There's a cobweb blowing in the heated hospital air. Somehow, it clings to the off-white wall, in the corner of the room I'm in. I can't see her, but I know Incy Wincy Spider is up there. She's trying to make things good and right in her world. She's holding on, despite all the shouting and pain in this room.

I feel just like Incy Wincy - tiny, blown about, clinging on tight to life. I've told them all once what has happened to me, but it won't be enough. I'll have to tell it again and again and again.

More police, more social. Court.

Me, lying here safe for a minute, safe from them - it's temporary. The police are outside my door. The on-call social worker is here. Tomorrow they will ask more questions.

I'm exhausted, but wide-awake. All I can think about is the climb ahead. How many times can I get washed down the waterspout and try to climb back up?

Someone brings me a small, plastic cup of liquid. It's to help me sleep, but I daren't take it. I can't trust anyone here to keep me safe, while I'm asleep. I lie there, so tired and so afraid. The route to resting is grasped in the cup in my hand, but I just can't.

I don't know how long I grasp that cup. And then Gail arrives. She's wearing pyjamas under her coat. Her hair is pulled messily back. She takes the medicine from the nurse, who is waiting with it, because he doesn't know what else to do.

"I'm staying here all night," Gail says. She moves a chair, so I can see her, from where I'm lying down. Then she sits, holding the little medicine cup in her hand. "I won't be leaving you," Gail says, looking right at me.

I'm so tired. I want to believe Gail, when she says she won't leave me. I know I should sleep, recharge my battery. I need to look like a grown-up, when they talk to me again, or I won't get Chloë back.

"All night," Gail says. She puts her fist to her heart and locks eyes with me. I look away. I tell myself, I feel calm, though I don't. I tell myself, sleep is part of climbing out of the waterspout. Incy Wincy Spiders need rest.

I nod at Gail - meaning yes, I will take the medicine. She passes me the cup. I hold it in my hand and stare at it. Come on, Incy Wincy.

I drink the medicine, then I wait.

I feel the texture of the pillow underneath my head. I know Gail is nearby. The medicine warms my body. Then it rocks me.

My eyelids droop and I drop into blackness.

CHAPTER 20

"Missie?" I hear a voice. My mouth is dry. My tongue still tastes of the sleep medicine.

"Missie?" I realise it's Isaac speaking – a nice doctor, who is here in the daytime. He is close by. He comes closer. Get back, Isaac. Too close. I sit up, ready to block him.

"It's okay, Missie," Isaac says, stepping further away. "I'm sorry, I'll stay here."

Daylight hurts my dry eyes, as I look around me. Gail Force is sitting in the chair, watching, like she promised she would. She holds her fist to her heart and looks at me. In my mind, I nod back at Gail, but I don't have the energy to actually do it.

"Missie?" Isaac is checking the chart at the end of my bed. "How are you?"

I can't answer.

"You've had quite a night," Isaac says. "Do you want to talk about it?"

I can't answer that either.

"She needs time," Gail says.

"And we need to get Mum charged and detained, before we have to release her," says another voice. It's Jemilah, the plain-clothes policewoman. This time she's with another woman, who is in uniform. They stare, like I'm an animal in the:

"Zoo, zoo, zoo."

Everyone looks at me, as if I've just spoken. Did I say that out loud? I think I did...

Jemilah and the other officer get chairs and sit.

"Missie, it's time to talk more formally about what happened to you and also about last night," Jemilah says. "We want to keep you safe and, to do that, we need you to make a full statement."

I want everyone to leave, so I can sit alone in the dark waterspout. I don't want to be stared at, in this harsh daylight. But I want to keep Mum away. And I never want to see him again. Or Nan.

"Let's do it," I say, sounding sure, feeling terrified. Chairs scrape, as people move closer. Social Sandra is here now too, with a notepad and pen ready. The policewoman in uniform clicks on the voice recorder and puts it on the table, which she wheels over my bed.

"Just as much as you can handle, okay?" Gail says.

"We need to get the full story today," Jemilah says. Gail looks at her. I wonder, are they going to argue?

But Gail just says, "Okay." She smiles at me. "You want me here?" Gail asks me. I nod, forcing myself to do it for real this time - I can't imagine making a statement without Gail.

Jemilah speaks for the voice recorder. Time, place, date, people in the room. I count, like I'm measuring the beats, before I jump in on a track. And we go.

"Can you recount for us the events of...?"

"How long had the abuse been going on?"

"How old were you when the abuse started?"

"Can you talk us through what happened when..?"

Different questions, same questions. Different versions of the same questions.

"Were you ever beaten?"

"What was your home life like?"

"Were your mother and grandmother aware of the things you were experiencing?"

It hurts – more than any broken part of my body hurts - to retell it. To relive it. To dig it all back out of me. Come on, Incy Baby Girl Spider.

My eyes sometimes flick to Gail, as I answer the endless questions. Gail is always locked on my face, never looking away, even at the hardest parts - where I have to talk about how Chloë got here. What he did.

While I am talking, I am running a background track in my mind. One of Chloë's nursery rhymes. I'm looping it, never letting go of it – it gives me courage to keep speaking my story out loud:

> *"So, the Incy Baby Girl Spider,*
> *Climbed up the spout again,*
> *The Incy Baby Girl Spider,*

Climbed up the spout again."

Over and over.

"Thank you, Missie," says Jemilah. I look around. Everyone's eyes are big, their faces shocked. I'm getting used to this reaction now, from these adults who are trying to help me.

"Am I finished?" I ask. The uniformed officer switches off the voice recorder.

Outside, I hear the sounds of the ward and the trolley clatters past. Is it dinnertime already? How long have I been talking for? Everyone gets up, except Gail.

"Can I see Chloë now?" I really need to know the answer.

Sandra looks at Gail, like they have spoken about this before. Then Sandra answers me:

"We're working on it."

"Working on it?" I say. "She's *my* baby."

"She's being well looked after," says Sandra. Gail stands and moves towards Sandra.

"We can't leave her here with nothing," Gail says.

"We'll be in touch soon," Jemilah says to me and leaves with the other officer.

"I'll get you an update on how Chloë is,

as soon as I can," Sandra says to me, looking at her watch, getting her coat and her bag.

Gail follows Sandra out of the room. I hear their voices in the corridor. They sound a bit like a whispered MC battle – each trying to get their point across.

Gail says loudly, "She needs some good news!"

I do. I really do.

As Sandra replies to Gail, their voices move further away from the door, until I can't hear them anymore. It's just me and Incy Wincy Spider. We're alone in the room now. Everyone has sat, watched me speak my pain, then switched off, like I'm a TV show.

I thought those words I spoke were me, scrabbling up the spout and getting Chloë back. But now, I'm doubting everything.

Maybe I will never get Chloë back, because they don't think I can look after her properly?

Maybe they're right?

Maybe I'm destined to live in the waterspout, washed out for all time? Never bothering to climb back up.

Maybe it's the end of Incy Baby Girl

Spider and her little Chloë Spider?

CHAPTER 21

With all the words washed out of me. With no Chloë in my future sight, I feel hollow.

I thought I would feel brave - like I was fighting for something – when I told my story. But I just feel weak. When no one knew how Chloë came, those parts of me were invisible to everyone else. But now people know and I feel so embarrassed.

Ashamed.

And my shame gets bigger, the longer we sit together. The two of us.

They offer me dinner on a tray - I ignore it.

Isaac brings in a young, female doctor and talks to her about my physical injuries, while I just lie here, listening to a list of my body's own failings.

After they've gone, I keep remembering the answers I gave, to the questions the police asked. Same thing, lots of different ways.

It presses on me, as I have been pressed on before – the weight of everything. All that scrabbling - rising up that dark, slippery waterspout to tell my story to everyone. But I'm still here alone, without Chloë and with no one letting me know, if I will ever get to be with her again.

I can't breathe. I can't pull in any oxygen.

As the cobweb blows, I no longer know if it's real, or I'm imagining seeing it here. Are you still clinging on there, Incy Wincy? Are you with me? Maybe I am you - that spider in a web. I'm not the broken person in this bed.

"Incy Baby Girl Spider,
Climbed up the waterspout."

I think of Chloë. I imagine she is here with me, listening to me perform for her. She smiles, one fang shining, drool running down her chin. I picture her wearing a cream, fleece onesie and white trainers with a gold swoosh.

I pull her hair up into a little topknot, with the cutest bobble. She sits on the bed, her hands in front of her, supporting her own weight. She is safe and strong and I don't need to worry about her falling off.

"Mamamamamamumumum," Chloë says, like the old days. She's rocking back and forth, which means, come on, carry on, more songs. I move my mind to how my phone screen used to look. I scroll through Chloë's nursery rhymes playlist.

I sing to her:

"Five little ducks went swimming one day."

I sing her the whole song, MCing my own words in and out of the soothing sounds:

> *"One day, you and me will be far, far, away,*
> *One day you and me, won't be swimming round this place,*
> *Let these grown-up ducks come quacking,*
> *Let them look, let them flap,*
> *We'll have swum, over the hill, to our own little flat."*

Chloë loves it.

"Mamamamamamumumum," she says - meaning more. I scroll further through the phone playlist in my mind.

"We're all going to the zoo tomorrow."

But, as I get into that, it makes me think of school. Of the normal teenagers. Of my friends who I've drifted away from and who've probably given up on me by now. I need a different song. I try:

"Oh dear, what can the matter be?"

But it makes me think of Nan and the salon. Of the okay days, that are gone now. Of the bad days - like when Mum spotted the Hold the Mic flyers and all the trouble for me was beginning to kick back off.

Another song comes to me on auto play - I'm no longer in charge of the playlist in my mind:

"How much is that doggy in the window?"

Mangy Mum Dog.

And now Chloë isn't all nice and bright and clean, sitting up happy and healthy on the bed opposite me. Now she is slumped in her buggy, strapped in tight.

Her big, scared eyes look at me, from a tired, blotchy face.

We are back there. I am back there.

"Go!" I shout. I get Chloë out of there, out of the place, of the pain, of my imagination. Just like that, she is gone. I can't see her anymore. And I am back in the hospital room.

Someone comes in. I am handed more sleep medicine. People hover, waiting to see what I will do.

I just take the medicine this time. Being asleep, is better than remembering.

CHAPTER 22

Gail is back the next morning. As I open my eyes, the bright light pours through the hospital room window towards me.

"I've been sitting in the waterspout all night," I say. Gail looks at me, like she doesn't know what to make of me. Then she looks across the room.

I see Social Sandra is here too. I wouldn't have spoken my thoughts aloud, if I'd known Sandra was here - I want her to think I'm normal, so I can get my baby back.

"Missie," Gail Force says. "We've come to talk to you about Chloë."

My heart starts to hammer in my chest. The palms of my hands feel sweaty. I rub them on the hospital blanket. The up-and-down movement makes my ribs, neck and left arm hurt – some of my shattered places.

"Tell me!" I want to shout, but daren't. Act normal, look like a good parent.

"I know you've been keen to see her," Sandra says.

Keen? I'm desperate. But I can't act it - in case they think I'm not normal - so I just nod, tense-necked.

Sandra opens her folder. She's printed out a picture of Chloë, on a piece of A4. "This was taken yesterday," Sandra says.

They've got Chloë in some horrible outfit, with a cartoon character on it, like an old person would dress her. She looks like she belongs to someone else.

I can't look at it. I feel like this is already over. Like my baby is moving on without me. I try to picture Chloë, in the cream onesie that I imagined, but my head's feeling hot. My mind's stopped working. My eyes sting with frustration. Stop it. Stop those tears. I don't want to cry right now.

I put the photo down. It rests on the bed, under my hand – the touch keeps me connected to Chloë, without having to see this new version of her.

I watch Sandra look at Gail. It's like a game of eye tennis in here. People need to speak, instead of all these eyes at each other, across the room. It makes me think of Nan's looks that mean:

"Keep your mouth shut."

Mum's looks that mean:

"Keep your mouth shut."

His looks, his points, stares, big, badman wolf energy – it all means:

"Keep your mouth shut."

Yes, I'm swishing and swooshing down the waterspout now, to the dark place, where they had me living so long. I have to get away from all the adults and their looks.

"It's too much for me."

Gail and Sandra snap their heads to look at me. Did I also say that out loud? I daren't ask. I don't have any power over myself, just like I don't have any power over this situation.

Even though I am a parent, I am still being treated like a child. But then, I am also behaving like one. I can't act normal any longer.

"Just tell me!" I shout.

Gail stands. She comes closer to the bed,

but not too close, and speaks gently, "Okay."

"No more secret looking at each other," I say, my voice sounding clear and certain. "I don't get what it all means."

I sit up, so I can see Gail and Sandra properly. I scrunch Chloë's photo in my grip.

Will I only ever have this photo of Chloë, to remember her by? I don't have my old phone with photos of her on. I don't have any others printed out. And now she's gone - and this photo is not my version of her. But still, it's all I have. So, I'd better treat it nicely.

I release the paper photo from my hand and press upon it gently, hoping I can uncrease it. No one looks at anyone else. I can't think of another thing to say that will help me. Then Gail blurts out with a question, "You wanna come live with me?"

What?

I look from Gail, to Sandra, to Gail, to Sandra - now, it's me doing the looking, to check if this is a joke. But Gail is looking only at me, directly – in that clear-as-glass way she has. Sandra is also watching only me, waiting.

Looks like it's my turn to speak. "For real?" I say.

"For real," Gail replies. I pinch my fingers together, to check I can feel the pressure of life upon myself. I'm not still asleep, am I?

"I don't understand," I say. Sandra stands too. She takes a couple of steps closer to the bed, on the other side from Gail and then speaks gently and slowly to me:

"Gail is a DBS-cleared youth worker, so we are able to rush through certain elements of our foster carer approval system."

I look at Gail. "Marcia's going to help us," Gail says. "My mum."

Yes, Marcia, the fostering pro. This makes a kind of sense, but still, I have a big question:

"Why?" I ask. "Why would you want me?"

"Why wouldn't I?" Gail asks quickly. She sounds cross. Oh no, I shouldn't have asked why. I picture the cobweb, to give me something to focus on. I'm messing everything up. I don't know how to act in these types of situations. I wish I could shrink to the size of a spider.

"You're amazing, Missie," Gail says. I am?

"And you deserve a safe home," Gail says. "You both do."

Both?

Chloë *and* me?

Does Gail really mean it?

"What?" I ask.

Sandra replies, "You and Chloë can both live with Gail, if you'd like to?"

Sandra's question hangs in the air - I can't think of a way to reply.

I can't picture a life, where me and Chloë are not alone and scared. Where we're not hungry and scratting about to survive. I can't believe anything good could happen to us. I shake my head at all these thoughts.

"You don't want to?" Gail asks. Her tone is neutral, like she's asking me a simple question, not a hard one.

I shake my head again, but I don't want Gail to get me wrong. I have to speak. I force a word out. "No," I say.

Gail's face crumples a little, though she holds it, stops it, like she's trying not to show it.

Wait. She doesn't understand what I mean, does she? I hurry more words out of me, quickly saying, "I don't mean no."

Gail waits for me to continue. How can I put it? I look at the ceiling. I picture the cobweb. Then I speak, "I don't know how to say yes." My words stay there, stuck just outside my mouth.

"You mean, you're confused?" Sandra asks, kindly.

Ah! It's so difficult to explain myself, when no one has ever asked me, given me any kind of a say in anything before.

How can I answer? How can I take a step, to a life that's not secrets and tucking myself in the corner of other people's spaces? I could say:

"Thank you." Or, I could say:

"I'd love to." Or, I could even ask a question back, like:

"How will it be?" But all those kinds of words are kind of lies - because I'm not that kind of person, that talks that kind of way.

"Are you interested in living with Gail?" Sandra asks, slowly. The question is more pressure. Sandra is trying to help, but it's the final button-press. I can't stop it. It comes...

I shrug.

I hate myself.

Gail and Sandra look at each other. Sandra speaks:

"Shall we come back another day?"

"Don't leave me here!" I say, my voice wobbling, so I sound like a little kid again. Everything is getting so messy, so embarrassing and it's all my fault. These people are trying to talk to me and help me and I don't know how to speak back.

"Please," I say.

"Let's take a few steps back in this conversation," Sandra says softly, then adds, "You'll soon be leaving hospital."

Stepping into the outside world? I can't picture what that will look like. I feel Chloë's photo crunch in my fingers again and I have to force myself to open my hand.

"It's been decided that you and Chloë are not safe at your grandmother's house, at the present time," Sandra continues. I nod. That is so true. Nan will open the door to Mum in a heartbeat, if we have to go back there.

"There are specialist units, care homes for young mothers and their children."

There are?

"You were probably told about them,

when you first had Chloë," Sandra says.

"No one told me anything," I say. "No one helped me." Gail speaks up:

"Well, we're going to help you now, whatever you decide, aren't we, Sandra?"

Sandra waits, as if she's deciding whether to answer Gail. But then Sandra speaks, straight to me, "The unit would be away from here, both for your safety, and also because there aren't many of them and places come up rarely. You may be a hundred, or more, miles from here."

A hundred, or more, miles away? What even is that? I can't picture it. It feels like another country.

But, maybe a hundred or more miles away, is exactly how far away we should be? Then he can't get to us. "Will he be able to find me?" I ask.

Sandra shakes her head. "We can give you a new identity, you and Chloë. When he comes out of prison, you'll be gone."

I would love to live in a world where he didn't. I try to imagine what it would look like. Me and Chloë on a park bench, or wheeling down a pavement, but everything around us is blank. It's a drawing with only two people in and no backdrop, no detail.

At least here, I have people I know. Gail and Marcia. My friends, if they still like me. Buildings, parks and streets I recognise.

I can imagine how that might be. I can see it.

"I want to stay here," I say. "I want to own my own life. And I want to be an MC."

Gail nods.

"You'll teach me, won't you?" I say to Gail, eye-to-eye with her. A picture of my future is beginning to form.

"You don't need any teaching, Missie," Gail replies. "You know more about writing songs than I do."

Does Gail really think I'm so good? I remember that night, what Gail said to me, After Hold the Mic, about being a true artist.

If Gail believes in me, perhaps one day, I can believe in myself?

But, still, why would she take that on? She has a great life – she doesn't need an abnormal teenager and her baby messing that up.

"Is that why you want us to live with

you?" I ask. "So I can be an MC?"

"Not - really," Gail says, dragging her words out. Gail looks at Sandra. Sandra gives Gail some kind of eye signal. Here we go with the eye tennis again.

"Stop it," I say. "Just tell me what you mean."

Sandra speaks first. "Gail has something to explain, Missie." Then, silence.

What?

I snap my head to Gail. Gail doesn't meet me eye-to-eye this time. She looks down. She's like frosted glass – she's not clear, like she usually is. This is making my heart bang.

"Tell me!" I shout.

Gail looks up and speaks. "I knew you," she says. I don't understand."What do you mean?" I say.

"I knew you. When you were little," Gail says. She unlocks her phone. Her shiny, gel nails tapping on her big phone screen – latest model.

Gail holds the phone out for me. She's showing me something, on the screen. A photo, but a vintage one. The colours say old-fashioned. The image isn't sharp. It looks like a photo of a photo.

First, I see a young Gail. Her hair is darker, scraped back, her make-up different, but I can see it's her. She is sitting on a hospital bed, looking happily at the camera, leaning towards a woman and a baby.

I know this photo.

It's the one from Nan's hall, where Mum's holding me – her new-born baby. The photo that is really small, like it has a piece missing. And now I know what's missing.

It's Gail. She was there. Just like she is here now. She is right next to Mum in the photo – they are touching.

"You're the other part of the picture," I say.

"Yes," Gail says. My ears are full of the sound of blood under pressure, a fast-beating heart that's pumping at its absolute limit. I can't look at this photo anymore - it makes me feel I don't belong in my own body. I push the phone away.

"Will you let me explain?" Gail asks.

Now I get it. All the looks. Gail and Sandra. Mum and Gail. Him and Gail. Secrets. I thought I was free of all that now. I feel sick.

"I'm your mum too," Gail says.

"Gail!" Sandra says, strongly. Gail looks down.

The room is full of feelings.

Feelings that are pressing me, pushing me, ragging me around.

I pull the covers over me – it's easier to breathe in my own air, my own space. I don't want to be out there, in the room.

I want to be alone.

"Get out!" I shout, from under the covers.

"Missie, please," Gail must is almost next to me, really close. I can't breathe with realising how near she is.

"No," I say, pushing my voice out through the sheets. Then, I can only say one more thing:

"Leave!" I yell. My voice hurts with how hard I've just shouted.

I can tell Gail is still there. I can't have her here. She feels like the biggest lie I've ever been told. I wrap myself tightly in the sheets, trying to get away. I start to sweat, which makes me feel even worse.

I close my eyes. I block my ears. I breathe

quickly, hot tears stinging my face. I stay there, wrapped up, hot and still. After many long minutes, I realise the room is quiet and still and empty. I look out from under the covers. They are gone.

My face starts to cool. I pull the bedding further down, letting more heat escape from the sheets round my body. But my mind is still trapped, wrapped-up.

That photo Gail showed me is burned onto my imagination. It's one lie, one secret too many. I'm done. Done with it all.

I sit up, my stomach clenching with pain.

My legs creak and screech inside. I'm damaged, but I'm getting up regardless.

I move, everything in me hurting. My middle feels like it could come apart, as I stand on a chair and reach up to the imaginary cobweb, in the corner of the room.

I feel like my hands touch it, even though I know it's not really there.

I bat my hand at it – the edges of the cobweb stick to me. I hit and swipe at it. I rub it away from my hands – onto the floor, onto my hospital gown. Away from me. Gone. Silly spider.

I move back to the bed, curl up on my side. I face away from the window, away from the door, away from the world. I'm done figuring it out and scrabbling up, coming back, fighting.

Let the rain come and wash me down for good.

CHAPTER 23

I'm swept down, into my days gone by. I'm little again and living in the dark.

So many memories flash by me, through me. I feel dizzy. I can't keep up. It feels like someone else is in my brain, swiping fast, through the images and videos, on my life's camera roll.

First, I remember some of the regular difficulties of my early years. The day-to-day stuff.

Mum leaving me at Nan's for weeks on end. Dumping me there - in the clothes I stood up in and not much more.

Me wondering, waiting – was Mum coming back today? Or the next day? Or the next week? I remember raindrops running down window glass, as I looked out for hours, hoping Mum would walk down the alleyway, heading to Nan's, to finally collect me.

I remember the pink of a new pack of pyjamas, wrapped in plastic. Opening them, for the first time, sitting on Nan's carpet. How scratchy the fabric felt, when I wore them that night, and Nan saying, "I'm not washing the damn things as well. I've spent enough time and money on you already."

I remember that sick feeling, knowing I was a pain and a nuisance, to everyone around me. How bad I felt, about causing them hassle and stress, by existing. By needing pyjamas.

I remember being very small. Nan and Grandad arguing about Mum. Grandad telling Nan, "Stop making excuses for her!"

Nan replying, "That's my child and I will never turn my back on her."

I remember Grandad's slippers, on the end of his legs, while I played on the carpet and he watched TV. I remember a long feeling of quiet, after Grandad died. His empty chair. Nan crying. Mum shouting. Pain and sadness all around us, like stale air.

I remember the big, badman wolf -

sometimes we'd be there, sometimes he'd be at Nan's, with his big legs taking the space where Grandad's slippers used to be.

He'd tread on my fingers, on purpose, then wink at me, as I played on Nan's clean carpet, or his filthy flat floor.

I remember Mum taking me by the shoulders, gripping me there - her fingers so tight on the tops of my arms. Mum's eyes would bulge. Her breath would sometimes stink. She would say to me:

"Stop getting under his feet."

"Don't be a nuisance."

"Keep your mouth shut."

I quickly learned to sit quietly, out in the hall of his flat, for hours, alone – even in winter, when a wet draft would blow under the front door. My pink pyjamas were getting short on the arms and legs by then. I tried to be as small as I could, to stay out of their way.

I remember sleeping on an airbed in that hallway, with a towel for a bed cover. I had a fake Barbie that Nan had bought me – the only toy I had at his flat.

Fake Barbie was sharp and uncomfortable to hold, but I hugged her all the same. Mum would come outside to tuck me in. She'd lean over me and say, "Keep quiet. Don't annoy Kyren, okay?" I would nod and force a smile that hurt my mouth.

"Good girl," Mum would reply. And I would believe that she really cared about me. And that, if I kept being good, Mum would be happy with me.

That's what I've always remembered – snippets. I don't know in what true order, because one ever mentioned anything that had happened before.

I stay in these past times for days - all the while, knowing I am stuck, broken - in the hospital bed I am lying in. I exist in the present, but I live in the past. I lie on my back, then my side, then my back again. The light through my present window changes to dark and light and back to dark again. Many times.

I'm awake. I'm asleep. And the camera roll in my mind swipes on and on and on - memories that belong to me, but which I am not in control of seeing.

I think about Incy Wincy. How could she be bothered to keep scrabbling back up that waterspout? It's easier, washed down, in the dark.

But, if I stay washed away, I will never know more. More about Mum. And Gail. Me. I will always be just the Baby Girl. The one who bad things happened to. And I won't have a tomorrow. And then who will help Chloë have a future, that's not like my present?

I sit up.

I swing my legs off the side of the hospital bed. I am high above the shiny floor. There are socks on my feet. My legs dangle in the air. I watch them. I swing them. I think of Chloë, swinging her feet in her buggy, while I walk behind her, pushing us both in rhythm to the:

"Tip, tap, buggy wheel squeak."

But it's me swinging my feet in the buggy now. I'm wearing socks, and my legs look short and chubby and smooth. I have shiny shoes - like the ones some kids get - with a T-bar strap, from a proper shop. I zoom out from my past, for a minute, to wonder – who ever knew I had shoes like that? Not me, until today.

The rhythm of the buggy underneath me

sounds mostly like when I push Chloë. But it's also different:

"Tap, squeak, roll, time to go home."

I am in my buggy, feeling that rhythm, as if it's all around me. I swing my legs in time to the buggy beat. And then I realise, someone is above me, speaking words to the rhythm, out loud:

"Tap, squeak, roll, time to go home."

We roll on some more and the person speaks again. Then they hum. Little me tries to twist round in her buggy and look up to see who it is. But the buggy hood is up and I can't see the face the voice belongs to.

The voice continues:

"Tap squeak, roll, time to go home,
This little piggy whee wheed all the way home."

I turn round again. The voice is familiar, but different. My hands on the present hospital bed below me, are my hands on the fabric of my buggy, in the past.

The sameness between little me and Chloë, swinging feet in our buggies, someone making MC nursery rhymes above us.

I let the rocking of my body drop me into a rhythm, like it does when I'm writing a song.

What other songs did I hear as a little kid? I shut my eyes – maybe not seeing today, will help me move through my childhood camera roll?

I'm in the bath. Tiny, shiny, white, foamy bubbles cling to my golden-brown legs. A smooth, light brown hand dips into the water and pours the gentle warmth over me. Am I me? Or am I Chloë?

The voice half-sings, half-speaks:

"Incy Wincy Spider,
Climbed up the waterspout."

I pull back, stop rocking, stop sitting in the warm bubble bath of the memory. That song? My escape route, when I was getting broken again by him? The shock of the similarity makes me pull breath sharply into myself.

Is this real? Was that song actually sung to me? I have survived to this day, and kept Chloë alive, by not looking at the past, by finding ways not to think about the things that have happened. But I want so much now to look up and see the face of the person who is singing that song to me. I want to zoom in to that picture on my camera roll and really examine it.

My breath is moving quickly in and out of me. I know I need to slow it down, to be able to control my swiping. I imagine the steady tempo of a bass beat, instead of being controlled by the rapid, treble section of a track.

Once I have the bass, I imagine I'm dialling down its pace. Controlling it.

Slow.

I rock my legs again, sending myself back to where I was, to the little me. I say out loud:

"Incy Wincy Spider."

I am back in the bath again. I move my hand on the hospital bed - I splash my hand down in the little-me bath. I hear the sounds of the ward, outside my room – I hear the splash of water, as I sit being washed. Someone rubbing my arms with bath bubbles, then rinsing the foam off. Someone sing-speaking:

"Down came the rain,
And washed poor Incy out."

I hum along – today and in the past, at the same time. I look at the bubbles. I look at the edge of the water. I look at the walls of the bath around me - they are white, with a little mark of grey, at the water's edge.

I look further and further up, towards the voice, which continues:

"Out came the sunshine..."

I follow the bubbles, up the long arm that connects to the voice. Then both golden arms reach for me. I am lifted from the bath. A warm, soft towel is wrapped around me. I nestle onto a soft and welcoming body.

Until today, I did not know I had ever been hugged as a child.

I feel the slow, happy pulsing of another human next to me – their chest upon mine. It makes me think of Chloë. It makes me think of how I feel, when sound flows into me and helps unlock words I can write to a beat.

Then the voice speaks again, to the heartbeat tempo we share:

"So the Incy Wincy Spider..."

I look up at the face that is smiling at me. She is younger. Her hair is darker, like the photo. She has a spot on her chin and a furrow in her brow. She locks her eyes on mine, in the same way she has, whenever she has come to see me. Whenever I have held the mic at The Lowdown.

It's Gail Force.

She finishes the song:

"Climbed up the spout again."

I slide from the height of the hospital bed. I feel my feet, in their socks, on the hard floor. I am stiff. I hurt. I have to shuffle and it takes all my energy. There are so many things broken in my body and mind, but I think of little me and Gail Force.

I think of Chloë.

And those things I'm thinking of keep me going.

I leave the room.

Out at the desk, in the middle of the ward, Isaac is sitting. He is writing in some files, a bright light shining over his papers. His eyes flick up. He sees me. He smiles. "Missie," he says, kindly.

"I..." My voice is so dried out. My throat feels like it's red raw, on the inside. Isaac gets up, as if he might need to catch me. Maybe he will. I feel weak. I feel like my legs could go any moment.

I have to do this, though. I have to bring my past and my present together. "I want to see Gail Force," I croak the words out of me.

Isaac nods. "Okay, okay," he says. He leaves his desk and offers me his hand to take. I look at it. "It's there if you need it," he says.

But I can't. I don't want to touch, or be touched. "Will you call her?" I ask.

"I will," Isaac replies, quietly.

We walk back to the room. Isaac close by,

ready, in case I fall. If I had any voice left, I would make noises with each step I take, because it hurts so much.

The room is now dark.

I lie on my side. Isaac is shadowed in the doorway, waiting, watching. The lights of the ward corridor shine behind him. I let out a long breath.

"I will get her for you," Isaac says. "But first, let yourself sleep. You need the rest."

Then Isaac goes, back to his desk, to his work and to looking after all the children.

I lie here, alone - a grown-up on a kid's ward, a girl who had a baby - until I fall down the cracks of myself and into sleep.

CHAPTER 24

It's morning. I see her, as I turn over - Gail is standing in the doorway. How long has she been there?

The rattling breakfast trolley is being pushed down the ward corridor. The clatter drowns Gail's voice out, as her mouth makes the shape of my name, "Missie?"

When I asked to see Gail last night, I thought I was ready, but I'm not. I turn to lie on my other side, facing away from her. I close my eyes again, but I can still see the recent memory of her shape, as the sun shines through my closed eyelids.

Gail waits. She doesn't hover and fidget, like Mum. She just is. I open my eyes again and stare at the blank wall, at the corner of the room. Why did I get rid of that imaginary cobweb? I've got nothing to pretend to look at now.

Gail asks, "Can I come in?" I turn on my back and look up at the ceiling, to let her know I'm listening – it's all I can manage.

Gail steps into the room. I hear her lift a plastic chair towards the bed. She puts it down softly and sits to the side of me. In my peripheral, I can see that she is wearing a black jumper. I see the tops of blue jeans. Her hair has been pulled quickly back – she looks less polished than usual. Gail-Not-Full-Force.

She waits and I listen to the beat of my heart – it's loud in my ears. All I can think about is that poor, pretend spider that I have left without a web.

"Incy Wincy," I say. Beat, beat, beat, goes my heart.

Gail Force replies, "I used to sing that to you. I used to sing them all. The old school, classic nursery rhymes."

I hear Gail sniff. She's reaching for a tissue, from the box on my bedside table. Then she stares at the floor. Is she staring away her tears too?

I put my hand out. It hurts to move my arm, but I can't leave Gail, alone there and so sad. My hand rests, light brown skin on the white, cotton bedsheet. Gail puts her fingertips on the edge of the bed. We are near, but not touching.

I notice Gail hasn't had her nails done and she's picked most of her old gels off.

Gail speaks her next words in a small voice. A sad voice. A way I've never heard her talk before, "They made me," she says.

I want to know what she means. I want to help Gail tell her story, the way she helped me when she could - she needs someone right now.

"Who did?" I ask Gail. "Who made you?"

"Belle," Gail says, her voice cracking.

I shiver – hearing Mum's name like that, from Gail's lips. It doesn't seem right. Mum's name means lovely – what a joke. Mum is the opposite of lovely.

"And him," Gail adds. "They both did it."

I stretch my hand towards Gail and turn my palm upwards. Gail walks her fingertips forwards, so we are touching, just a tiny bit - the slightest feeling of her skin next to mine.

My throat is stretched tight with the effort of trying not to cry. My voice sounds squeaky, as I say, "Tell me."

"Belle and me," Gail says. "We loved each other."

"What?" I say, not believing it. Mum loving someone as kind as Gail? Gail loving Mum back? Not possible. I shake my head.

Gail squeezes my hand, saying, "I know. It's hard to believe, but she wasn't always like she is now. She was really something, back in the day."

"I know how pretty she was," I say.

"Oh yeah, she was. But she was so much more than that," Gail says. "We were friends, for so long. Since college days. I worshipped her."

Mum? On a pedestal to Gail? "*She* should've worshipped *you*," I blurt out, quickly.

"Ah, Missie," Gail shakes her head. She taps her fingers on my hand. "Everyone loved Belle. All the girls wanted to look like her, to be friends with her. All the boys wanted to, you know. Every day, we walked in the refectory at college, the heads turned to follow and all eyes were upon her."

Wow. I bet those same heads look at Mum now and thank their stars they didn't turn out the way she did. The way I don't ever want to be. I can't see this picture of Mum that Gail is painting. There is nothing like that, in my mind's camera roll.

Gail continues, "She was such a prize to him. He was jealous of everyone. He'd had a bad life and he wanted what we all had. Love, security, something of his own." Gail drops her head, "So, he picked Belle."

I twitch, at the mention of him – the intruder. I curl up, move my hand away. Gail notices and asks me, "Shall we carry on another day?"

I'm desperate to know more, but terrified to find out the rest. I don't want another bad night, my mind's camera roll swiping through itself, the room's shadows creeping towards me.

"Tell me," I say out loud. "Don't say his name, but tell me. I have to know my story."

Gail nods. She sits back in her chair and I am glad of more space between us. Gail carries on talking to me:

"Belle was drawn to him. She couldn't stop herself. She knew he was bad, but she had some bad in her too – not in a criminal way, in a vain way.

She was jealous and greedy and selfish – even though she was so beautiful. He made her feel like he was the best thing that ever happened to her and no one else could give her what she deserved."

I listen. I force myself to hear only the words. I don't want to see pictures. I imagine I'm hearing text from a history book. Like a lesson at school - once I've learned it, I can forget all about it. It's just something I need to know for now.

Gail continues, "He'd been offending since forever, even in the days he lived under Marcia's roof. One day, he got put away for a few years. It was after we had left college and the garage music scene was starting to bubble. Belle started hanging round us all again."

Gail goes quiet for a while, then she says, "We became an item. Belle and me."

It's still blowing my mind. How could someone as kind as Gail, be with someone as mean as Mum? I can't imagine it. "What was it like?" I ask. "Being together?"

"It was amazing," Gail replies. "We didn't flaunt it. Times were different - much, much harder for two women to be a couple back then. But all our good friends knew. In time, we were living together, performing together..."

"Performing together?" I ask. I'm so shocked to hear Gail say that Mum performed.

"Yep," says Gail. "I was the producer, the MC, the DJ and Belle was the singer."

Okay, wow.

Gail continues:

"We were called Knight & Gail – Belle's surname, plus my first name. I can show you some old flyers some time, if you like?"

I shake my head. No, I don't want to see any flyers. I won't believe it, even if I do see them. I can't. This is too much. The past I didn't know about is pressing on me, like I've been pressed on before. I can't get enough breath in, so I have to breathe harder each time – quick and quicker snatches of air.

Gail stands up. "Missie?" She's leaning over me. The breath is leaving me as quickly, as it's being drawn in. Gail looks blurry. I feel like

I am sinking into the bed. I feel like I'm back in that room again, with him. Like the rain is lashing down the waterspout and washing me far, far away.

I feel Gail's hand on me, lightly, gentle. "Sloooooooow," she says. "Breathe. Out. Slowly..."

I hold carefully on to the next breath that leaves me, controlling it, under Gail's guidance. Gail's hand on my arm helps me feel like I am where I am - today, here, in hospital.

"Slowly, let it out," Gail says, making a sound, "Shussshhhh..." The air leaves her mouth slowly too. I try to keep my out breath in time with Gail's.

"Good," Gail says, quietly. "Shussshhhh." We keep going, until I'm back in charge of the air moving in and out of me.

Gail starts to sing to me:

"Incy Wincy Spider,
Climbed up the waterspout..."

I listen to her. It's lovely:

"Down came the rain,

And washed poor Incy out…"

I mouth the words with Gail:

"Out came the sunshine,
And dried up all the rain,"

My voice joins Gail's, as we whisper the last part together:

"So the Incy Wincy Spider,
Climbed up the spout again."

We stay like that a long time, Gail leaning over the bed. It must hurt her neck and her back, but Gail doesn't let her discomfort show.

Every time, the dark weight comes back upon me, Gail tells me, "Breathe. Out. Slowly. Sssssssshhhhh."

I lie there. Gail hums. It soothes my head. It helps slow my heart, which is beat, beat, beating in my tight, stiff chest. After a while, Gail's hum changes, to a different nursery rhyme tune - This Little Piggy. She switches it up, to the tempo of her own, old school, UK MC rhythm:

> *"This little piggy whee, wheed all the way home,*
> *You little Missie are no longer alone."*

My name, in Gail's song like that, it surprises me. I sit up, pain burning my ribs and stomach.

"Lie back down," Gail whispers, trying to help me sit back. I push her hand away. I need space. And freedom.

"No," I say, clearly - no squeaks, no scratches, in my voice. "I don't want to rest."

I want to know something more, about my life, about my story, not just Mum's and Gail's. I hardly know anything. "Why am I called Missie?" I ask.

"I gave you your name," Gail says, smiling. "I was the biggest Missy Elliott fan." Gail nods and points at me, "I knew you were greatness, like Missy, the minute I held you in my arms."

Gail knew I was greatness. I pull up the image of my newborn photo, in my mind's camera roll – the version with Gail in it, where she belongs. I want to know so much more about myself. "Was I born here?" I ask.

Gail nods, "Pretty much directly underneath this room."

My mind is racing.

Breathe.

How could they rub Gail out from my life? How might things have turned out for me, if Gail stuck around? My breath starts to quicken, as my thoughts get entangled within themselves.

Think slower.

Breathe.

I work to control myself, letting air out of my nostrils, as gently as I can. I feel lost, stuck, in half a story. I need to know the rest, but I don't know how to ask. I want to know why everything ended, with Mum and Gail. Why I never saw Gail again, growing up.

I need to ask Gail a question, that's breaking my heart just to think about. I treat it like a lyric. Let the question beat in my mind. Jump in on the track – 1, 2, 3, 4:

"Why did you leave me?"

Gail's eyes get big. I want an answer, but I don't, I really don't. But I do. I feel bad for pushing her and I feel scared to know, but I ask for more. "Please tell me."

"Belle, she went back to him, the next time he came out from jail." Gail speaks, slowly at first, but then the story begins to tumble from her:

"We had you, we had a flat, we had a good life, a career, though I had to work full-time as well to support us, but, she still went back to him, in the end." Gail takes a moment, then continues, speaking quickly, like she's only got one breath left:

"He was raging mad that it was me that was with her. He hated me, because I was adopted by Marcia and he wasn't and all sorts of reasons, but that's a whole other story. He was mad at Belle for getting pregnant to someone else – she didn't even know who, or that's what she said – but that is also a whole other story. He'd lost all his money, all the stuff he'd stolen and fleeced from people, before his last time in prison. He was skint and feeling crap about himself and he decided to make himself feel good, by ruining me. First he took

Belle, then, one day, he sent her for you."

I remember Mum, coming to take me and Chloë from Nan's, this last time. Was it a scene like that? Like Nan letting us go?

"I fought and fought and fought," Gail says.

Nan didn't fight for us at all.

Gail is still talking, so I force myself to focus my thoughts away from Nan. I'm back listening to Gail:

"Courts. Police. Going round with a baseball bat. I even tried to buy them off – but he just took the money and laughed in my face. In the end, I had to accept it." Gail looks down at the floor for the next part. "You were lost to me," she says. "They'd won."

Gail is bent low in her chair, hunched over. I feel for her. And I feel for me. They split us apart? How could they? No one else wanted me and Gail did. She fought? I thought no one had ever fought for me.

Turns out, I could've had a whole other life.

"I was broken," Gail says. "I went to work with a friend in America and ended up staying there. I was working on music, working with kids and young people, teaching them. I stayed in touch with Marcia and that was about it. I cut myself off from everything I used to know. I was heartbroken."

I feel my own heart squeeze, watching Gail, listening to her talk about her pain and sorrow.

"I heard you had a baby. At 15. I was so shocked."

Gail shakes her head. "I wanted to know how your life was, if I could help you. I wound my business up and came back to see what I could do."

Gail stands up and goes to look out of the window. "My goodness, when I saw you and Chloë, outside the library. I'd only been back a short while. You were so young and so old, all at the same time."

Gail leans on the windowsill, looking out. "What a little unit you were. The two of you," Gail says, quietly.

"We're not anymore," I reply.

Gail comes quickly to the bed, staying a foot away from me, not crowding me. "We can change that," Gail says. "Let me help you both. Let me make it up to you."

"Make it up to me?" I say. Gail's face crumples. She steps back.

"I'm sorry," Gail's eyes start to water. "I know I let you down."

I can't have this.

"No, Gail," I say. "There isn't anything you need to do, or make up to me." I push through all my pains to sit up and swing my legs off the bed. I'm not sure I can bear the contact, but I feel Gail needs it.

I hold both my hands out. Gail approaches and places her hands under mine, supporting my weight. "You haven't done anything wrong," I tell her.

And then, because I want to help Gail, I admit it to myself. I say it into the room. I take back my own story.

"They took joy from me, you from me, Nan from me," I say. I place my feet on to the hospital floor. I am weak, but I know Gail is ready to catch me, if I can't keep standing on my own.

"I'm getting my baby back. They're not taking her from me," I say. Gail nods. I lean a little into Gail's body. We are touching, just slightly, shoulder-to-shoulder. Only for a moment. And then I pull back. That's enough. No more contact. Still, we connected.

And it helps me, the connection, to become certain of my next move.

"Let's do it," I say. Gail waits, for what I am going to say next.

I point out to the ward. "Please go out there and tell them I want to go. I want to leave with you and get Chloë back."

"You sure?" Gail says.

"Hell, yeah," I say back, like we're at Hold the Mic and I know the same words everyone else knows this time.

CHAPTER 25

I go to Gail's the next day.

Gail has a bag full of pills from the hospital, to help keep my physical pains away, and a list of appointments for me, in her phone.

Isaac walks us to the steps outside, even though his pager bleeps at him to go be elsewhere. I want to say to him, thank you, but I can't. The words are stuck.

"See you soon, Missie," Isaac waves, as our cab pulls up.

In the back of the car, I feel soothed by a soft, fleece trackie and a puffa coat, that Gail brought me to wear.

Gail sits in the back with me, a hand between us on the seat. I feel her closeness, but she isn't touching me and I don't want to touch her. Loud music plays from the front. I put my hands over my ears - I can only handle beats in my head, not real life crash and boom right now.

Gail leans forward and asks the driver to turn the tunes down. Will I ever want to listen to music through speakers again?

The roads of the town roll by. But all I can think about is Chloë. What will she be dressed in? Will she be happy to see me? Am I still her Mamamamamamumumum?

We pull onto a small street, filled with little brick houses, all shiny and new. Gail gets out of the cab, as it stops. The glossy front door, of a neat house, opens. Marcia. She's smiling at me. It's so nice to see her face.

She has a small person on her hip. Their skin tones are two ends of the brown scale – Marcia dark brown and glossy, Chloë so light brown, her hair wispy, baby golden, with that touch of red. His hair flashes quickly, across my memory. I blink it away. Gone. Chloë is golden only.

Marcia points me out to Chloë. She takes Chloë's arm and waves it gently at me, saying hello. I feel like Chloë looks unsure. Does she cling a little closer to Marcia? I try to smile back, but I'm so weak, I don't know if it even looked like my face moved a muscle.

I start to regret being so bold, so sure - thinking I could come here with Gail and start something new and safe with Chloë.

The smooth, grey pavement under my feet is not a kind of surface that I recognise. The window blinds on the house, showing the inside of a smart, white living room. This is not my world.

I thought I'd made the big move, when I told everyone the truth about what had happened to me. But it turns out, that was one big move of many.

I feel I'm back to being trapped. I don't have a choice, but to keep moving. I couldn't stay in the hospital and be scared all the time, alone. I couldn't go to a care home and be scared all the time, about him coming for me. I couldn't wait and hope they would find a place for me and Chloë to be together. I knew I would be on a long list of girls like me – other Baby Girls, washed down other waterspouts.

I am standing outside a house I don't know and Chloë looks older and more grown and happy in Marcia's arms. What can I give her, that they can't? Gail and Marcia would look after her. I could just go - walk off, walk away, walk into nothing.

"I can't do this," I say, quietly. Then I feel the careful, light touch of a hand on my shoulder.

"Just step forward, then hold your baby," Gail says.

Is that really all I need to do right now?

"You can do it, Gail says. "I've got you."

One step.

"Take another step," Gail says, encouraging me.

Two step.

I think of some lyrics:

"One step, two step,
I'm almost at Gail's door."

Chloë reaches for me. She leans out of Marcia's arms. "Mammamum," Chloë says. She knows me. I'm so happy she still knows me.

And she's shortened her word for me? Did I hear that right?

I hold my aching arms out, as far as I can

manage. Marcia slowly passes Chloë to me, but keeps holding her underneath, taking Chloë's weight, so I don't have to – I don't think I could.

Chloë's grown. She feels stronger. Or am I just weaker? I wobble, as I think about how fragile I am. Gail puts a gentle hand on my back, to steady me.

Chloë pats my face. Her fingers are covered in drool. "Mammamum," Chloë says. Yes, her name for me is shorter now, and I can tell she means Mamma for sure. She looks at me, waiting, with her big eyes. I know what she wants. I touch my head close to hers and I say:

> "Incy Baby Girl Spider,
> Went down the wrong way,
> But she stopped and climbed back up,
> And now she's here to stay,
> It's so nice to see you, Chloë,
> Haven't you grown big?
> Now we are here together,
> We can climb up anything."

Chloë flaps her arms. She squeaks. She loves my nursery rhymes, the same way she ever did.

"So happy to see Mummy," Marcia says.

"They're happy to see each other," Gail adds.

I look at Chloë's hand on mine. It makes me think of Gail's hand, pouring foamy bubbles over my skin, when I was little – when I was Gail's baby girl.

I realise, my arms are shaking. I can't hold Chloë anymore. I'm feeling out of breath. I have to give her back to Marcia. Gail puts my arm over her shoulder. She takes my weight and slowly leads me into her sparkling house.

This is the type of place I used to dream of, when I sat among the trash and ash and tins, in that flat. I wished I could take Chloë to a fairy tale cottage – and now here we are.

Does that mean I am walking into my dream come true?

Does that mean everything is going to be perfect?

I breathe deep.

I have no idea how to live in a fairy tale.

CHAPTER 26

My life is fully lyrics:

> *"Incy Baby Girl Spider*
> *Was kicked down waterspout,*
> *The big, badman wolf wanted Incy gone,*
> *He wanted Incy out,*
> *But Incy Baby Girl Spider,*
> *Climbed to live another day,*
> *There was Chloë Incy Spider now,*
> *So Incy Baby Girl stayed."*

That's what I do. I write these little pieces of songs, short bursts – I can only think for a tiny amount of time. Other than that, I stare at Gail's TV, or sit at her table - pushing Marcia's lovely, home-cooked food round my plate, waiting for someone to take it, scrape it, away.

Chloë has a highchair now - she 's not just strapped into her buggy 24/7 anymore. The highchair is bright white and shiny metal, like the rest of Gail's kitchen. It has a tray Chloë pats with her hand, when she knows food is coming - pat-a-cake. I feel happy for Chloë, in the lovely highchair, but, at the same time, I feel shame that I couldn't buy it for her myself.

At mealtimes, I find it hard to eat, to swallow, to allow food in. Meanwhile, Chloë can't stop munching, making up for all the meals she's missed. "Mmmmmmmmm," she says, multi-coloured slops of dinner, oozing down her dimply chin.

Sometimes, I sit in a warm, bubble bath Gail has prepared for me. I shiver, even though it's not cold. I'm still, my arms wrapped around my broken bones. I don't want to stay in the water, but I don't dare to get out.

Meanwhile, Chloë splashes and sings through her own happy bath time, with Gail or Marcia, every night.

I can't settle. I don't feel like I have a place anywhere.

Meanwhile, Chloë is right at home.

One night, as I leave the bathroom, I hear Marcia and Gail talking in the kitchen. I stop. I stand, still, on Gail's landing. I strain my ears to hear what they're saying.

"Let her be, darling," Marcia says, speaking in a slow, deep way, which makes her easy to hear. Gail is more quick, like a popping instrumental - I can tell the feeling, snippets of the meaning, of what Gail is saying:

"Talk to someone... Too long... Needs help."

"She's got help," Marcia replies. "She's not ready for that other stuff, sweetheart."

Gail says something back to Marcia - it sounds like she is disagreeing. I hate the way their voices are not in synch, the way they clash. It's my fault they are not blending well. They're not in harmony.

I creep back to the small room I share with Chloë. She's asleep, smiling and smooth-faced, in her cot. I pull the pillows over my head, curl up, block out the sounds.

I think up some lyrics, to distract myself:

"Oh dear,

What can the matter be,
Me, causing them,
To fall out,
And to disagree,
Why? Am I here?
Bringing pain,
To their family,
I don't belong anywhere."

I repeat the last line over and over, in my mind:

"I don't belong anywhere."

I fall asleep, thinking it:

"I don't belong anywhere."

When I wake up, the lyric is still looping in my head:

"I don't belong anywhere."

I watch telly, push food round my plate, curl over in the bath. And all the time, I'm thinking:

"I don't belong anywhere."

CHAPTER 27

One day, I'm pretending to watch a TV programme about building houses, but I'm really drifting nowhere, in my head, like the clouds passing outside Gail's patio windows.

The doorbell goes ding!

Loud, clear, a surprise that makes my heartbeat skip and my breathing quicken.

Gail is changing Chloë, on a mat, on the carpet. She looks up towards the door.

"Who could that be?" Gail says to Chloë, who is more like Gail's baby these days, than mine. Gail scoops Chloë up and stands.

"I thought you could use a visitor," Gail says to me.

What?

Who?

I feel my body tighten. I feel the painful places, where I was broken, flare up - like a scab that just got knocked off again.

My heart beat, beat, beats.

Gail goes to the door. I stand up. "Who is it?" I say. My voice sounds dusty, because I hardly use it. Then she's in the room - I smell her lotions and products, before I see her.

Shannon.

She smiles at me. A big, open smile. Like we saw each other only yesterday.

I'm so shocked that she's here, I act weird. "What do you want?" I say.

"I wanted to see you," Shannon is still smiling, even though I've been rude. "Only for a few minutes. I won't stay long." Shannon coos at the baby - Chloë, a little star, grins back and squawks at her.

Gail puts Chloë in her buggy. "Good to see you," she says to Shannon. "We'll go out for a walk," she says to me. I feel lost and out-of-place. I just don't know how to respond.

I shrug. Exactly like Mum would've done in my situation. I am turning out just like her. And now I hate myself more.

Gail nods, like she doesn't care about the

shrug, like she hasn't even noticed it.

Gail and Chloë leave and there is silence.

I want to run and hide upstairs, but I don't want to be rude to Shannon. I sit on Gail's sofa, facing away from Shannon, who sits in the armchair.

"Oooh, it's nice here, isn't it?" Shannon looks around, at all Gail's fancy stuff. It is nice here. Too nice for me. I write another verse of the song in my head:

> *"Oh dear,*
> *What can the matter be?*
> *It's scruffy,*
> *And scratty,*
> *And tired and broken me,*
> *My friend's come to see,*
> *Come to chat,*
> *And be close to me,*
> *But I don't belong anywhere."*

I stare at the grain of the leather of Gail's cream sofa. I notice all the patterns, the swirls, how clean it is. It gives me something outside myself to think about.

Shannon puts a flyer on Gail's coffee

table. "It's for you," she says. "Everyone wants to know if Baby Girl is going to hold the mic." I don't look at the flyer - I know it's going to be something unrealistic, about going to The Lowdown and normal teenager stuff. I'll rip it up, when Shannon's gone.

"Missie?" Shannon says.

"Yes?" I feel shamed inside, by how rude I sound. I wish I could stop myself being like this.

"I didn't know, if we're still friends. If you hate me - for calling the police." Shannon is looking at her hands in her lap.

Wait? Shannon is blaming herself, for what happened? No.

"Shannon," I say. I hold my hand out. Shannon lays her soft hand in mine. It feels safe – I forgot how it feels to be near Shannon. I forgot we've held hands, since we were three. We held hands, while I kneeled, howling, on the hospital floor, trying to stop Chloë coming out of me.

Shannon is crying. Big, sad tears drop from her eyes, onto the pink leggings she's wearing. I hold her hand tighter. "Shannon," I put more feeling into my voice, more intention.

I really want to speak these words, so she can hear them:

"You saved my life."

Shannon looks at me. I squeeze her hand and tell her, "You saved Chloë's life too."

Shannon's pineapple bun wobbles, on the top of her head, as she speaks, quickly, "I didn't know if I'd made everything worse. Got you and Chloë in trouble. You were away for so long and no one would tell me what was happening."

Poor Shannon. Left in the dark. Blaming herself, when she should be praising herself.

"He hurt me," I tell her. "A lot."

Shannon nods.

"He was going to kill me, I think," I say.

Shannon nods again, dabbing her tears away. I stare at her wobbling pineapple bun, her shiny hair - anything to distract myself from the memories that are returning.

It's not working, though. My chest is getting tight. My breath quick.

I feel closed in. I feel like there's no air in the room. I stand.

Shannon stands too, instantly, like she is mirroring the teacher, in dance class.

"That's it," I say. "I can't tell you anything else right now."

"Are you coming back?" Shannon asks. She's got a look, like she is trying not to cry more. She used to get it all the time, when she was still learning how to lose, or get criticised, in her dancing competitions. She'd get a rush of tears, fight them back, and her face would wrinkle, as she forced the tears not to return.

I know Shannon so well. I know how she looks soft, but she is so strong and determined. Thinking about Shannon, tough on the inside, helps me to feel stronger too. Strong and determined to tell the truth. To speak, from now on.

I don't want to make Shannon feel more sad, but I'm not ready to walk back past Nan's. I'm not ready to go to school and hear shouts of "Baby Girl." Maybe I never will be.

"I don't know if I'm coming back," I say, honestly.

Shannon and her bun nod. I feel tired, with all this emotion and these memories I am trying not to look at. I yawn. Shannon takes the hint.

"I'll go," she says. She picks up the flyer

again and puts it in my hand, before she leaves. "No one holds the mic like you," Shannon says quickly.

And then she is gone, hurrying away, closing Gail's front door, with a gentle click. I watch her, from Gail's front window. Small, quick steps. Her back perfectly straight.

I look at the flyer.

HOLD THE MIC – LIVE

Shimmering, gold text on black paper. Gail and the crew are putting on a night at The Lowdown.

There are prizes – cash and time in a recording studio. There are DJs. The slick design of the flyer has a pull on me. I wish I could go, in another life, where I am a normal teenager.

But no. I just can't. What would I MC about? How I've been broken? How I was almost killed? No one wants to hear that.

I go upstairs. I slide the black and gold flyer under the pillow, then lie on the bed. The looping lyric returns:

"I don't belong anywhere."

CHAPTER 28

A letter comes. From the courts. About testifying.

The paper flaps quickly – my hand is shaking that hard.

The page is full of words that are moving around upon it. My chest feels tight. I try, but fail, to draw quick breaths. Before I know it, I'm on Gail's sofa, my head bent over my knees.

Gail is rubbing my back, saying, "Breathe. Out. Slowly. Sssssssshhhhh."

She repeats it, just like she did at the hospital. Gently, she takes the letter from me. "I'm kicking myself for not being in when this came." She tucks the letter away, in her pocket. She sighs. I think of the old ladies, stuck in the lavatory, in a proper fix. Sighing, in that old lady way:

>"*Oh dear.*"

"I'm stuck in life's lavatory," I say out loud to Gail.

"What?" Gail asks, quickly.

I've started now, so I may as well continue:

> "*Oh, dear,*
> *What can the matter be,*
> *This letter proves,*
> *I am stuck in life's lavatory,*
> *Don't get flushed away,*
> *Have to stay,*
> *And my pain repeat,*
> *These people,*
> *You know,*
> *They don't care.*"

"Some people do care, Missie," Gail says, gently.

I listen to her, as she explains:

"I care. Marcia cares. Shannon cares. Derren cares and Tommy cares – those two are always asking about you."

"Are they?" I'm surprised. Derren and Tommy? I thought I would have drifted into their past, like they've drifted into mine.

"Well, Derren asks about you and Tommy nods, mostly," Gail says.

I believe her.

Gail carries on, "Sandra cares. The people, who looked after you in hospital, Isaac, the police. They all care. They've made their lives about caring."

This is quite a big list.

"Everyone's behind you. We're with you. You don't have to do it on your own," Gail says, then she stands and walks to the bottom of her stairs.

"Come with me," she says, nodding upwards, to the place where Chloë is napping.

The stairs creak, as we creep carefully up them together. Gail puts her finger to her lips:

"Shussshhhh..."

We're outside the room I sleep in with Chloë. Gail pushes the door open, swoosh across the carpet. Gail points in at Chloë. The baby is sleeping on her back. Arms up, mouth open, skin smooth.

Gail takes my hand and whispers, "Chloë cares."

I watch Chloë's chest rise and fall. I think of myself, at Nan's, on her spare bed, waking up where I'd fallen asleep in my uniform, watching my baby girl rise. That part, at the start of the day, was the most precious thing to me.

Chloë saying her special word that meant me, "Mamamamamamumumum."

The way she would wake and grin at me, through the travel cot mesh. How she would look at me, as I would stroke her cheek and smile for her, always hiding my daily fears. How she would lock eyes with me, while we hid in the corner in his flat. Me willing Chloë to sleep in her buggy, to keep her safe.

"I am her mum," I whisper.

"Yes, you are," Gail whispers back.

"He's got nothing to do with her," I say.

"No, he hasn't," Gail says. "And he never will."

I want to be with her. I want to be with my baby. I want to hold her and look after her. I know best how to do it. I know the songs she likes, the way she likes her buggy pushed. I know how to make her laugh and how to soothe her to sleep.

"I want to do it," I say. I enter the room properly, approaching the cot. Gail creeps back downstairs and I wait to I hear the lounge door close, before I get really close to my sleeping baby. Chloë is wearing soft clothes – fleecy, cream joggers and a light grey top. Her face is changing - from a baby to toddler - just like mine is changing - from a teenager to an adult.

I bend down. It hurts, where my cracked ribs are healing, but I push through it.

I scoop Chloë up, holding her weight in my broken, bent and bruised arms. The pain flashes in me. I feel it, like I feel the memories of everything that's happened to me. It's always there.

How will I do it? How will I move us both through my pain? I feel my breath quicken, my skin warm up, with the worry. Chloë snuffles and starts to wake. Soon she will open her eyes, re-booted, after a sleep – I wish I could do that.

I smell her. I feel like I'm holding all the times I've held her. When they first put her in my arms, in a hospital room full of shocked faces. When I got ready for school. When I sang for her and was her personal MC. I have tried to be a good parent. And I put Chloë first.

That means I'm not like Mum.

Chloë opens her eyes - dink. She looks at me. She pulls her head back, like she wants to see me properly. I'm too weak and hurt to keep holding her. I sit with her, on the bed.

Chloë reaches a chubby hand up. I lower my face and she touches it. "Mammum," she says. Shorter, again - almost a proper word.

Chloë is me and I am Chloë. The sound of her speaking vibrates in my body. I am standing next to the speaker at The Lowdown and the bass is humming in me, like it used to. The first words of one of Chloë's favourite songs come out of me:

> *"The wheels on the bus go round and round."*

Chloë smiles and squawks. She shuffles, ready for more, like, come on, Mammum. I imagine the song playing from my phone, as it used to and I jump on the imaginary beat:

"The wheels on the bus go round and round,
Just like our lives living round my home
town..."

I pause, then quickly think of the next
section:

"I'm back now with you living in our brand,
new home,
I promise I won't leave you all alone, alone,
alone."

Chloë squeaks with happiness. She
wants more. I hug her tight to me. "Eeeeeee,"
she says. I tickle her. She giggles.

"Round and round and round," I say.

Chloë is the other half of me. She needs
me. And I need her. We have to stick together.

But how can I do it? How can I get us
both back up that waterspout?

I think it through, while bouncing Chloë
on my lap to entertain her.

I can't do it alone. I've tried that.

I will need to change - ask for help.

I think of Shannon. I think of Gail. I think
of Marcia, Sandra, Derren, Tommy. The official

people. Isaac at the hospital. All rooting for me.

I'm tapping my foot, as I name everyone, to the spider's nursery rhyme track:

> *"Incy Baby Girl, list them,*
> *There's people who'll help out,*
> *There's others who have got your back,*
> *Who don't want you to drown..."*

Chloë giggles on my knee, tee hee:

> *"You can see the sunshine,*
> *You can climb from your pain,*
> *Me and Chloë Incy Spider,,*
> *We'll keep climbing every day."*

It feels so good to make a song - to stitch lyrics and music together, like I am also stitching myself together. I have written songs in my darkest of times. And I'm going to keep writing them, until I am back in the sunlight again.

Chloë is waiting for me, for the next bit. She is my biggest fan:

> *"Mummy and Baby Spider,*

They are getting out,
They slid right down into the dark,
But they are rising now,
They are digging in,
And reaching out,
And learning who to trust,
My Incy Chloë Spider,
It's always the two of us."

Chloë reaches up for my face, "Mammum," she says. I hold her close to me, but my legs are shaking, from the effort of jiggling her about, to the music I was making.

I lie Chloë down on the bed, where she rolls onto her side. The Hold the Mic Live flyer shines, sticking out, from under the pillow – black and gold. Chloë spots the shiny flyer too and pulls herself forward, to make a grab for it. I take the flyer quickly out of her reach – I don't want her to cut her mouth on it.

"Look Chloë," I say.

"Mammum," Chloë's reaching again, for the flyer – it's so shiny, she really wants it. I move it from her reach and grab a soft teddy rattle for her. The black and gold flyer shines in my hand.

Can I?

Dare I?

Go to Hold the Mic Live?

Like Shannon asked me to?

I lift Chloë up again and stand up with her. It hurts to hold her weight alone. I know I should put her down, that my body is asking me to stop. But I have to do one more thing. If I'm going to go to Hold the Mic Live, I have to tell Gail now, before I change my mind. Before I tell myself I'm not normal and it's not for me.

Gail's making lunch in the kitchen. I hand Chloë to her, my arms shaking and tired. Gail moves a kitchen stool under me and I sit, dropping onto it - no longer able to hold the weight of my weak, wobbling body.

My muscles are cramping. My heart is working hard, pumping. I slap the Hold the Mic Live flyer down, on the clean, grey worktop.

"I'm going to do this," I say.

"Okay," Gail nods.

Chloë is patting Gail's face. Gail moves Chloë's hand gently down, so she can speak to me, asking, "You sure?"

I'm not sure, but I guess I have to become sure, by acting sure.

"Yes," I say – I'm surprised by how clear, how certain, I sound. There's no crack in my voice.

"You're a wonder," Gail says. "You know that?"

I don't know that – and I don't know how to answer that. Gail is looking at me, like she's waiting for an answer. I feel that family shrug rise in me. It's climbing up.

Chloë points at me and shouts, "Mammum!"

No, I think. Go shrug, I think. I am not paying Gail back for everything with a stupid shrug, like Mum or Nan would. I'm not showing Chloë the family shrug and passing it on to her. The thought of the words I am about to say feels so strange, so uncomfortable, but I force them out:

"Thank you."

I accept the compliment.

Gail grins, then puts Chloë in her chair, giving her a stack of soft, buttery fingers of bread to munch through. I watch Chloë grab the bread, mush it about in her hands. She gets some of it into her mouth and most of it all over her face.

I feel like I have finally arrived here, at Gail's, to start the next chapter of my life. Gail gets on with making lunch, throwing a question over her shoulder, as she works:

"What song are you going to do?"

I have no idea. I didn't think beyond getting down the stairs with Chloë and announcing my intention to Gail.

So now, already, I have a new dilemma.

What song am I going to do?

CHAPTER 29

I'm sitting on Gail's sofa, staring at the new phone Gail has given me. Gail is out. Chloë's in bed and Marcia's looking after us.

What song am I going to do?

What song am I going to do?

What song am I going to do?

Shannon adds me to a group on this new phone Gail bought me. Tommy and Derren are added too, and the chat is flowing between them, like it's my old days.

SHANNON:	Excited for Hold the Mic Live.
DERREN:	when we gonna practise?
TOMMY:	See you soon.

I become fully convinced that I never

should've said a word about Hold the Mic Live. I don't know how to answer my friends. How to interact. How to pretend. I know they're trying to be friendly, helpful, show support. But I can't meet them back with the same energy.

SHANNON: What song's everyone gonna do?

Oh no. I don't know. What do normal people say in abnormal situations? How can I reply and just get on with this thing, move forward?

I look at Marcia, who has fallen asleep. Marcia is the most normal person I know. Normal with me, when no one else knew how to be - making that small talk in the salon chair, about Chloë. All the kids Marcia has fostered, the trouble she must have had with him, but she's still someone you can have a conversation with. Normal.

How can I be more like Marcia? What can I give my friends, without giving myself away? How can I be nice to them, without having to tell them anything? I unlock the screen. The phone is warm in my hand, as I open the group.

MISSIE: *typing...*

I hesitate.

MISSIE: *typing...*

I keep it short.

MISSIE: See you there

I switch my phone off and put it under my bed. I want to forget it's there. More questions - more chat - will come and I don't have anything else to offer right now.

I keep my phone off until Friday - the big day.

I stay quiet and just play with Chloë and watch TV and go to bed early, for the rest of the week. Gail doesn't hassle me. She doesn't even mention Hold the Mic Live. I don't hear a beat, or get an idea in my head, only the question:

"What song am I going to do?"

I lie on my bedcovers, listening to the sound of Marcia arriving to babysit. I hear Marcia and Gail downstairs, low voices talking.

Chloë's bedtime programmes playing on the TV.

I get my phone out from under the bed. Am I ready to switch it back on, and jump back, into that normal teenager life?

I hear Gail's footsteps on our soft, stairs carpet. She knocks once and my door swooshes open.

Gail pops her head into my room, around the door. Her hair is up in a curly bun. She is wearing a plum lipstick and her golden skin shimmers. She puts an arm out. She is holding a hanger of clothes.

New, black leggings.

Crisp, white t-shirt.

New, denim jacket.

Like a new version of the old me.

Gail hangs the clothes on a hook, at the top of my door. She places a fresh pair of black and white pumps on the floor, inside the doorway. No one has ever bought me nice things - things that suit me, things I want to wear.

Be normal, I tell myself.

"Thank you," I say.

"Just come and watch," Gail says. "No

287

pressure." She has big hoops on tonight, hoops the same gold as her coat. She is Gail Full Force. She shines, where I feel dull. But, I want to show her that all her work means something. That I need her. That I'm trying.

"I'm going to do it," I say.

"Okay," Gail says. She smiles at me. I need Gail to understand something. And I know she won't be able to, unless I use my words and explain it to her.

"I'm going to do all of it," I say. "Hold the Mic, going back to school, the court."

Gail is listening.

"I'm going to write an album," I say. "I've got all these bits of songs I wrote in my head. Before." I'm breathing quickly, rushing to get the idea out.

"I'm going to pull them all together. I'm going to call it Nursery Rhymes."

I gather energy and air into me, to speak my last words:

"I'm going to make something of me and of Chloë. Of our lives."

I stop talking. All the ideas, the plans, my announcement – it's all now real and in the air around me. I've spoken it and Gail's heard it. Does that mean, it's kind of starting to happen?

"I'm here for it all," Gail says. And I know I believe her. I know she will help me do the things I've said I want to.

One day, I will ask Gail so many questions. About her. About me. About Mum. But, for now, I have to stay in this minute, in today only. The future and the past are too big, either side of me.

"One step at a time," Gail says, as if she knows what I'm thinking.

"One step, two step," I say. Then Gail points to her watch and grins, "Can you be ready in ten, though?"

I laugh. A tiny laugh, but my first laugh in a long time. One step, two step.

"Chloë's coming too," I say. Gail looks as if she might be about to speak, to say no.

But then, Gail tells me, "You're the boss."

And she's right. I am. I am Chloë's Mammum and I know I will always do my best for her.

Gail returns downstairs, leaving me to get ready. I quickly put on the clothes that Gail's bought me. They feel soft – of course – on my skin. They smell of our clean house. They smell of me being cared for enough, that someone thought to buy me clothes and wash them for me and bring them to me. It's a new sensation and I really like it.

Downstairs, Marcia has her coat on and Chloë is snug in her buggy, dressed up for the night air. I feel excited. I feel scared. I feel like we need to get moving, so I don't change my mind again.

Gail has the buggy handles in her hands and she is pushing Chloë past the coats hanging in our hall. I think of Nan, always taking over. Those days are done.

I step forward and speak, "I'll do it."

"Of course," Gail says, moving back to let me through.

I take the buggy handles. I walk ahead, wheeling Chloë. She is mine and I am hers. I like being in front of Gail and Marcia with the buggy. I feel like, in choosing where I place my feet, how I wheel Chloë forward, I am choosing our future.

We pass the alleyway to Nan's house. I see her curtains drawn, her TV lights flickering.

I imagine her watching telly. I picture

her drinking wine, eating fish and chips. I face away from Nan's, look forward and move on.

The Lowdown is buzzing. Lights and music flow from the building. People are talking, gathering outside, filing in. I feel myself slow on the approach, like I used to, worried the crowds won't part, worried someone will shout out:

"Baby Girl!"

But slowing down means the idea of his flat, on the far side of the square, gets bigger in my mind. I know he's not there, but I feel like the light is on outside his door. Like he is watching, waiting, gripping the balcony.

Gail tells me every day, "He's in prison, until you testify. And he's in prison after that as well."

"Come on, Incy Baby Girl," I think to myself. And I keep moving forward with the buggy.

I see Shannon – she's leaning on Tommy. Derren's close by, rocking to the beat that's coming out of The Lowdown. They see me back. Shannon waves. I wheel towards them and put the idea of that flat to the back of me.

Chloë's feet are tapping on her buggy -

she can feel the beat like Derren can. The crowd at the bottom of the path to The Lowdown are tight, busy, noisy.

"Baby Girl," someone says, like it's a fact. Here we go.

"That's right," Derren announces. "Ding, ding! Here she is."

And no one else makes any further comment.

We go up the path - Chloë, me, my friends. Gail and Marcia are behind us. Everyone is now following us into the building - they were all waiting for Gail to arrive.

I take a minute to think about how lucky I feel for once, to have Gail back in my life. Our lives - Chloë and me.

"What song are you going do?" Shannon asks me, as we wheel through the crowd within, to find a space at the edge, for Marcia to sit and mind Chloë's buggy.

I can't answer.

Shannon says it again, louder, thinking I haven't heard her, "What song are you going to do?"

Don't shrug, I think.
Breathe.

Out.

Slowly. 1, 2, 3.

"I don't know yet," I reply loudly back.

I look around, buying time to think. People are performing already. The crowd are a bit into it. Being kind, but not bugging out. Nothing too amazing is happening so far.

Gail stands by the DJ. She catches my eye and signals to the stage, like, "You coming?"

Breathe. Out. Slowly.

I have to go for it. I will run back out of The Lowdown, if I don't go up and hold the mic right now.

I nod to Gail and she gives a thumbs-up and points me out to the DJ.

But I freeze. I'm stuck. I'm halfway up the waterspout and the rain has started coming again. I'm seconds from being swept back down to the bottom.

Marcia is leaning down, to unclip Chloë from her buggy. Derren and Shannon are dancing, grinning at me. Tommy is next to me, watching them. He asks me a question, "What do you need?"

I remember, I have to ask for help now, if I want to move forward.

"Can I borrow your phone?" I ask. Tommy passes me his phone, no questions. I see a picture of Shannon and Tommy on his wallpaper. They really are a proper couple and I am glad about that.

I search up a track online - the track that I climbed my way out into truth with.

Gail waves at me across the room and speaks into the mic:

"Here's someone you've all been waiting for, since she first held the mic, months ago."

I feel like I know, and I don't know, what I am going to say, when I hold the mic. What song I'm going to do.

I walk through the crowd, towards Gail. I imagine the track that I'm thinking of, is slowly rising in volume in my mind. People smile, tap me on my shoulder, move to let me pass. I do recognise a lot of these faces, from Hold the Mic. From before.

No, don't think about that.

I let the volume of the track in my mind increase. I imagine it pushing the other thoughts out, taking over.

The lights are playing all their colours in the dark. I am sweating so much, I feel like

Tommy's phone could slip and slide from my hand.

I reach Gail. She holds her palm up for a high-five. I am so weak with nerves, I tremble, as I pat her hand weakly back.

The DJ salutes me, like we're old friends. I try to smile back, but my mouth is so dry with worry, that my lips stick to my teeth.

Gail nods, gesturing for Tommy's phone. My hand is shaking so much, I clumsily drop the phone into Gail's hand. Gail looks at the screen, takes in the track, nods and passes the phone to the DJ. The DJ nods at me, then plugs in the phone. I watch the DJ mix my track in, with the heavy bass beat that was playing before.

Am I really going to play a nursery rhyme, a baby song, in this Hold the Mic Live situation? In front of everyone? In front of all these people?

Wait. Near Gail, by the wall, is that Isaac? And Sandra? They came for me? Wow.

But all these people, all this pressure. What if I freeze on stage?

The plink, plink, plink of the beginning of the track is coming through. There's still a space behind me, where the crowd parted to let me pass. It can only have been seconds, since I walked through them. But it feels like years.

I look back. I see Marcia standing. I see Chloë in her arms, reaching out a hand to me, her lips making the shape of "Mammum."

Gail, Marcia, my friends, Isaac, Sandra - all these people are around me - the people who I know have me and want to help me. There will never be a better time to hold the mic. Never, in my whole life.

I feel the space between Chloë and me. There's too much distance. We're not going to be parted again. I run back to Marcia, the plink continuing to rise in the track. I have to jump on it soon, or it won't sound right.

"Mammum," Chloë says, as I reach her. Chloë leans out of Marcia's arms towards me. I take her weight. It hurts me still to do so, but it's getting easier. This is all getting easier, so I need to keep going. Keep climbing.

Chloë is rocking excitedly. I walk back through the space that was made for me by the crowd, holding my baby. Gail is there, still waiting, mic still out.

At last, I hold the mic.

I grip it tight. It feels alive, like it could jump from my hand.

People whoop. They are cheering me on. They are here for me.

I walk up on the stage, with my baby in my arms.

The light shines on us. Chloë and me.

I look out into the crowd. I see Shannon and Tommy are holding hands. Derren is swaying to the beat. Marcia is now standing with Isaac and Sandra. Everyone is smiling at me. I feel their energy. The way they are wishing me on.

I speak these words like lyrics, hard on the beat:

"I'm Baby Girl."

The next plink, plink - of the track I know so well – is rising. Breathe. Count the beat. 1, 2, 3, 4.

"I'm going to do a song about an Incy Baby Girl Spider," I say.

Now, Chloë is holding the mic too. I hitch her close to me.

I jump on the beat. I start my song.

We climb up the waterspout for good.

ACKNOWLEDGEMENTS

I wanted first to acknowledge all the MCs, writers, poets, musicians, producers and other artists out there, making things happen, creating work in challenging situations. Even if you can only take tiny steps towards your goal, keep going.

Special mention also, to all the young people I've been fortunate to work with over the years – you've provided me with so much inspiration - thank you.

To the colleagues who work supporting and encouraging our young people – you make a big difference and you are appreciated.

Specific gratitude to Jo Walker – the designer of the wonderful cover of this book. You brought Missie and Chloë to life and did a beautiful job. I'm delighted we worked together.

To the team at New Writing North –

you've made all the difference to my writing career – thank you so, so much.

Special mention to Will Mackie, for epic levels of support and encouragement.

Thank you to the generous and kind, Lisa Williamson - guest judge when Baby Girl won a Northern Writers' Award and gracious and giving of her time and support many times since.

To the people in the publishing industry, who expressed interest in the book, and offered both encouragement and advice, thank you all.

A huge thank you to my friends, family and colleagues, who urged me along the epic journey of writing and preparing to independently publish Baby Girl. Thank you for showing interest in the book, many of you long before you got to read it. You helped me dig in and keep it going.

Finally, to my husband and my son - you are everything to me and I am so thankful to you, for all you do to help and nurture me every day.

ABOUT THE AUTHOR

I am mixed-race Indian and White British. I grew up in a stormy household, in a vibrant and varied part of London, where difference was a cornerstone of our community.

We later moved to a part of Yorkshire where difference was not celebrated - but more about that in my next book...

Since the age of 14, I've had over 100 jobs, including salad washer, editor, checkout assistant and actor.

These days I work as a writer, producer, director and facilitator. I love telling stories for and with children and young people in books, theatre, online and in film-making.

I wrote the first draft of Baby Girl on my phone, commuting for my full-time job. I wrote the next five drafts at my dining table at weekends, early mornings and after work. If you want to, you can do this too.

Thank you for reading Baby Girl. More information about me and my work can be found on my website:

emmahillwrites.com.